D0504604

For the first time man and soldier were at odds as desire warred with duty.

He liked this woman, he wanted her physically, but if she was of the royal family his duty was to protect her against all threats—including himself. With the addictive taste of her still on his lips, he recognized the challenge that represented.

He knew his duty—lived and breathed it day in and day out. Duty was what kept the soldier from kissing her when she so obviously wanted a kiss as much as he wanted to get his mouth on her. The shadow of hurt as she moved away drew the man in him forward as he sought to erase her pain.

And his.

Now might be the only time he had with her—this time of uncertainty while the DNA test was pending. Once her identity was confirmed she'd be forever out of his reach...

Dear Reader,

In my Princess Camp stories, I've enjoyed writing about every little girl's dream of playing princess. Rapunzel must risk all she's ever known and the safety of her isolated tower to seek the freedom she longs for above all else. Her reward is finding a family she never anticipated and a love beyond all imagining.

This story reminds me of my lovely niece Sammy. She started in softball at the tender age of four and by the time she was ten she and her team won Nationals. Hard work and dedication brought her many more honors and last year she finished a college softball career that broke many individual, school and division records.

What is her connection to Rapunzel? Sammy is a beautiful blond with hair that reaches past her waist. This past summer she was recruited to play professional softball in Italy, Sammy left all she knew to travel to a foreign land. Because of her long, blond hair, the people of Italy called her Rapunzel!

Isn't life funny sometimes?

Enjoy the journey.

Teresa

THE MAKING OF
A PRINCESS

BY
TERESA CARPENTER

MILLS
BOON

First published in Great Britain 2013
by Mills & Boon, an imprint of Harlequin (UK) Limited.
Harlequin (UK) Limited, Eton House, 18-24 Paradise Road,
Richmond, Surrey TW9 1SR

© Teresa Carpenter 2013

ISBN: 978 0 263 23491 6

Harlequin (UK) policy is to use papers that are natural, renewable and recyclable products and made from wood grown in sustainable forests. The logging and manufacturing process conform to the legal environmental regulations of the country of origin.

Printed and bound in Great Britain
by CPI Antony Rowe, Chippenham, Wiltshire

Teresa Carpenter believes in the power of unconditional love, and that there's no better place to find it than between the pages of a romance novel. Reading is a passion for Teresa—a passion that led to a calling. She began writing more than twenty years ago, and marks the sale of her first book as one of her happiest memories. Teresa gives back to her craft by volunteering her time to Romance Writers of America on a local and national level.

A fifth generation Californian, she lives in San Diego, within miles of her extensive family, and knows that with their help she can accomplish anything. She takes particular joy and pride in her nieces and nephews, who are all bright, fit, shining stars of the future. If she's not at a family event you'll usually find her at home—reading, writing, or playing with her adopted Chihuahua, Jefe.

Recent books by Teresa Carpenter:

BABY UNDER THE CHRISTMAS TREE
THE SHERIFF'S DOORSTEP BABY
THE PLAYBOY'S GIFT
THE BOSS'S SURPRISE SON
SPARKS FLY WITH MR MAYOR
SHERIFF NEEDS A NANNY

Did you know these are also available as eBooks?
Visit www.millsandboon.co.uk

For my editorial team at Harlequin Romance
past and present. Thank you for your patience,
encouragement, and insight. We make a stellar team.

PROLOGUE

Princess Camp

AMANDA CARN SHRUGGED INTO her backpack then grabbed the handle of her rolling suitcase. Slowly, reluctantly she followed her roommates and new best friends from the cabin they'd shared for the past two weeks.

She'd had the time of her life here at Princess Camp and she wasn't ready for it to end. She'd never be ready for it to end.

"Amanda, come on." Michelle, a bouncing blonde dressed as Sleeping Beauty, waved her along. "If we don't get to tea early, we won't get to sit together."

"I'm not hungry." She winced at the petulant note in her voice. She detested petulance.

Grandmother's displeasure came across as petulant, and oh how she would hate it if she knew. A professor at an elite Northern California University, she was a brilliant woman, disciplined in both manner and emotion. She rarely allowed a show of temper, which was a good thing, because it wasn't a pretty look on her.

"Well, I'm starved." Elle, beautiful as Belle, gave Michelle a significant look and they both came back to hook an arm through each of Amanda's, drawing her forward.

"I'm going to miss you guys," she whispered, not wanting it to be a whine.

"I'm going to miss the scones," Elle declared. "Hurry."

"Our time's not up yet, silly." Michelle told Amanda, refusing to be rushed. "We have the tea, and then the closing ceremony. There's lots of time left."

Something in her voice made Amanda turn to study Michelle's profile. "You don't want to leave, either."

"None of us want to leave." Elle sighed, brushing her mahogany curls behind her. "But I don't want our last day to be sad either." She stopped on the path and turned to face them. "We have to all promise to come back next year." She held up her hand, little finger raised high. "Pinkie swear you'll do everything you can to come back."

Michelle immediately hooked her pinkie finger with Elle's. "I'll start working on my dad as soon as I get home. He owes me for missing parents' day."

Amanda's hand curled into a fist as sadness bloomed into despair. "It would have been better if my grandparents didn't come to parents' day. Grandmother has already said she felt the camp misrepresented itself as having a curriculum of etiquette and decorum when it was clearly a production of fantasy and frivolity."

Her friends blinked at her.

"You mean she doesn't like the camp because they let us play princess while teaching us manners?" Elle said.

Amanda nodded. "I doubt I'll be able to talk her into letting me come again."

"Is that why they only stayed an hour on parents' night?" Michelle asked.

"No." She worried the end of her long strawberry blond braid. "They had another engagement. Grandmother was hosting a reception for a visiting professor. They have them all the time."

"She couldn't do that another night?" Michelle demanded, reaching for Amanda's hand. She, too, knew how it felt to come second to duty.

"It doesn't matter. I would have been nervous if they'd stayed for the talent show."

"Afraid Grandmother wouldn't approve?" Michelle guessed.

Amanda shrugged, feeling it would be disloyal to agree even if it was true. She longed to come back next year. Her grandparents were very protective of her and the university life was restrained and structured, with not much to offer a ten-year-old. And Grandmother didn't like it when Amanda made a fuss about things.

But then some things were worth making a fuss over. Like precious friends. Looking from Elle to Michelle, Amanda slowly lifted her hand and hooked her pinkie with theirs.

"I promise to keep in touch. And to do everything I can to be here next year."

CHAPTER ONE

Fifteen years later

XAVIER MARCEL LEDUC, Commandant of the Royal Pasadonian Republican Guard was ready to go home. For six months he'd been away, traveling with the crown jewels on an extended American tour that started in New York and would end here in San Francisco.

He ran his gaze over the well-dressed crowd. Tonight was a pre-event viewing, for the social elite and members of the museum, and privileged donors. Hardly a high risk crowd. All the more reason to be on guard, in his opinion. And as the senior officer in charge of the crown jewels' security, his opinion counted.

He saw her the moment she walked into the room, a breath of fresh air in a throng of perfumed elegance. She wore a black ruffled skirt that ended a few inches above her knees topped by a black sweater with beaded trim. Young and chic, her only adornment was her creamy white skin and the vibrant fall of red gold hair that reached the top of her lovely derrière.

An attractive blond accompanied her through the exhibit, but it was the redhead who held his attention. Not only was she lovely, something about her was familiar.

When the women reached the portrait of Princess Vivienne, he went totally still, the hair on the back of his neck standing on end.

Signaling one of his men to take command of his post, Xavier approached the woman and her companion.

"Oh, oh, oh. Look how the tiara sparkles. That's it. I just decided I'm having a tiara for my wedding. Do you think you could borrow this one for me?"

"Shh!" Amanda hooked her arm around Michelle's and drew her away from the delicate diamond display. "These are royal jewels on loan from Pasadonia. I do not work for this museum, so no, I can't borrow it for you. Now behave yourself."

"I guess I could just snatch it."

"Oh my God."

"Relax. I'm just teasing. Trying to get you to relax. You're bound tighter than your grandmother's knickers."

"Stop. And no more talk of borrowing or snatching any of the Crown Jewels. That's not going to relax me. Security is all over the place. It would not look good to the museum I do work for if I was kicked out of this one."

"Is it the security that has you twitching?"

"No. I mean it shouldn't be. We're not doing anything to draw their attention. But I feel like I'm being watched. It probably is the extra vigilant security."

"Maybe not. Let's take a gander, shall we?" Michelle led the way to one of the three foot by three foot glass displays that stood six feet high in the middle of the room. This one held a beautiful ballgown from the late 1800s topped by a stunning ruby necklace, earrings, and tiara.

Being women, the jewels got first consideration but the elaborate dress also drew Amanda's attention. "Can you imagine wearing something that heavy to dance in?"

"I couldn't do it." Michelle shook her head, her blond hair

shimmering with the motion. "I would have had to be a strumpet."

"Ha." Amanda closed her lips over a burst of laughter, the old habit hard to break even though she'd been out from under Grandmother's iron rule for nearly six months. "I'm telling Nate you said that."

Her friend slanted sly green eyes her way. "Nate loves my inner strumpet."

"I bet he does." Amanda bumped shoulders with her best buddy. "I'm so happy for you. It's obvious you two are in love. He's been good for you."

"Dude, he's the best. And he comes with the little munchkin."

She glowed. The biggest cynic Amanda knew actually glowed talking about her fiancé and his infant ward. It made Amanda ache with delight for her friend, but also with loneliness.

Both her BFFs had found their very own Prince Charmings. And Amanda truly wished them a fairy tale happily ever after. But it made her long for a man of her own, someone she could be herself with, who would believe in her without limits, who loved her despite her faults.

Despite her faults? Wow, she had to stop channeling her grandmother. She wanted what she'd never had, a relationship of comfort, warmth and affection. She longed for a man she could trust, a man who above all else would be honest with her.

And yes, a man who embraced her inner strumpet.

"There he is," Michelle whispered in her ear. "Your stalker."

"Where?" Amanda looked up and into the brown eyes of a black-haired man. He stood militarily straight, on the edge of the room, arms crossed over his chest, eyes trained on her.

She smiled. And he quirked an eyebrow.

She blinked and looked away, pulling Michelle with her towards the display of royal portraits.

"Mmm, sexy," Michelle observed. "And he definitely has his eye on you."

"You were right, he's security. Head of security for Pasadonia."

"How do you know?"

"I saw him on the morning news. They were doing a piece on the opening. He's part of the Pasadonian Royal Guard traveling with the crown jewels."

"He sure is pretty, but intense. It looks like a smile might break those cheekbones."

"Don't stare."

Amanda pulled Michelle around so they faced the painting of a woman wearing a three-point crown and a jewel encrusted crest around her neck. The plaque read Princess Vivienne, 1760–1822.

"He's working." For some reason Amanda felt compelled to defend him. "And some people like to kid around about stealing the tiaras."

Michelle grinned. "Bet that would land his ass in a wringer."

"Yes, actually, that is indeed the truth."

The deep male voice with a slight accent sounded from behind them causing Amanda to jump guiltily.

Michelle was unfazed. Smiling easily she turned to confront the man. "You can't put all these sparkles on display and not expect a girl to want."

"You are welcome to admire all you wish." He bowed his head slightly. "That is, of course, the point of the tour. However, I must insist you do nothing to place my ass in a wringer."

Amanda smiled appreciating his humor, the gentle mocking.

"Oh, he's funny." Michelle took no offense. She elbowed Amanda. "Sexy and funny, you should say hello."

"Hello." Well used to her friend's bluntness, Amanda just went with it. Besides, he was sexy, and funny. She held out her hand. "I'm Amanda Carn."

"Miss Carn." He bowed low over her hand, almost but not quite kissing her fingers. "It is my pleasure."

Michelle shifted so he wouldn't be able to see her, and wiggled her eyebrows. Amanda just stopped herself from rolling her eyes. But she couldn't help but be charmed.

"Xavier Marcel LeDuc at your service."

"You must forgive my friend, *monsieur*. She has a warped sense of humor but means no harm."

The Commandant nodded to the portrait behind her. "Your resemblance to Princess Vivienne is what drew me over. Do you, perhaps, have family in Pasadonia?"

"Oh my gosh," Michelle exclaimed. "Amanda, you totally look like the princess in the picture."

"What?" Amanda automatically turned to view the painting.

The woman in the picture appeared to be in her forties. She wore her bright red hair up, the weight of it, and the crown making her long neck look fragile. A creamy complexion and somber blue eyes gave her an elegant air. She possessed a delicate beauty beyond anything Amanda aspired to. Yes, their coloring was similar, but that was all, and even then Amanda's strawberry blond hair and silver gray eyes resembled the woman's but were a toned down version of the princess.

"Oh no." Amanda automatically made the denial. Because really, the closest she got to royalty was playing princess at Princess Camp all those years ago. But then she had to qualify, because she didn't really know her full ancestral makeup. "Not that I'm aware of."

"The likeness is quite remarkable."

"Oh please," she gave a dismissive wave, "she's beautiful."

"Yes." He nodded, a shallow, regal gesture, his amber gaze never leaving her face. "Very beautiful."

"Oh." She blushed. Those compelling light brown eyes held her captive, seemed to delve into her soul, seeking all her secrets. And she was keen to share. Michelle's elbow dug into her ribs, reminding her to speak. "Um. Thank you."

"What she meant to say," Michelle corrected, "is would you like to join her for a cup of coffee?"

"Oh I cou—" Again the denial came without thought, but she stopped. Why couldn't she? She wouldn't find her prince charming by being timid. "Yes, I meant what she said."

He smiled, not with his mouth but with those incredible eyes. "This would be my wish, however, duty requires I remain here."

"Of course." Heat rushed to Amanda's cheeks as his rejection registered. "You're working."

"May I have a rain coat? Perhaps tomorrow morning?"

"Rain check," she gently corrected him. "I'd be delighted to meet you in the morning. There's a decent coffee house two blocks from here."

He inclined his head and they agreed on a time.

"Ladies, may I take your picture with Vivienne's portrait? A memento of our meeting."

"Of course." Michelle gave Amanda no chance to answer. Hooking her arm through Amanda's, she smiled as Xavier held up his phone and took the shot. After which he bowed and excused himself to return to work.

"You have a date with a foreign hottie," Michelle chortled as soon as he stepped out of ear shot. "I'm so proud of you."

"It's only coffee." Amanda down played the date, because she didn't want to get too excited, even though her heartbeat drummed wildly and her palms were sweaty.

"It's a date with a sexy, sophisticated man. And you don't fool me. Inside you're dancing on tiptoes."

Amanda shook her head. But this was Michelle, so she finally came clean. "I totally am. Which is probably a huge mistake." She gestured to the displays around them. "The exhibit is only here for six weeks."

"Exactly. No time to get emotionally attached, but plenty of time to have fun. And if you're lucky, you might get to celebrate your freedom with a foreign hottie in your new apartment."

"That's your inner strumpet talking."

Michelle laughed. "You're right." Her gaze went to the painting of Vivienne. She looked from the picture to Amanda and back again. "Are you sure you're not related to anyone in Pasadonia?"

"Not on my mother's side. They're Norwegian."

"What about your father? You don't know what your dad was. He could be Pasadonian."

"Michelle, we're not talking just anyone in Pasadonia." Amanda pointed at the painting. "She's the Prince's great grandmother. We're talking the royal family."

"I know. Cool, huh?"

It was her turn to laugh. "Yeah right. I'm the long lost daughter to the Prince of Pasadonia."

She had to scoff because they'd just tapped into one of her biggest childhood fantasies. She'd loved playing princess and often pretended to be rescued from her lonely existence by a prince who took her away to his beautiful castle.

Her mother had died from complications in childbirth, so Amanda was raised by her grandparents, who were in their late forties when she was born. They always maintained they didn't know who her father was, that her mother never revealed his identity.

"Hey, your mom may have met him when he was on a trip to America. Or she could have had a European trip after college."

"If she did, I've never heard of it." Amanda sighed. "They rarely talk about her. Grandmother gets so withdrawn when I ask questions. I stopped asking long ago."

Michelle muttered an unflattering word about grandmother and then wrapped Amanda in a hug. "Sorry, but I've never liked her since she refused to let you come back to Princess Camp. Plus, I know what it's like to be in a stifling home situation. You do know Elle and I love you."

"Yes, I do know." Amanda squeezed her friend before stepping back. She'd been taught from birth to avoid public displays of affection. "I love you guys, too. But enough of this silliness. I have a date with a foreign hottie."

"Yes, you do." Michelle went with the change of subject. "What are you going to wear?"

"Oh no, you're not going to do that to me. I'm not going to go mental over what I wear tomorrow. That's your thing, not mine."

"I don't know how you can be so calm about such a big decision. Impressions matter."

"I'll be fine. I don't own anything that won't make a good impression."

"Yeah. Now that you're out on your own, we have to do something about that."

"Sir?" Officer Bonnet appeared at Xavier's side in answer to his summons.

"See the redhead leaving with the blond?" he indicated Amanda and her companion. "I want you to follow her. Discreetly. I want to know where she goes, what she does, and where she lives."

"Yes, sir." Bonnet turned to leave.

"Bonnet." Xavier stopped the man. "Don't let her see you."

"Sir." Bonnet nodded and moved after the women.

Xavier watched Amanda, she moved gracefully, her posture straight, elegant. It wasn't hard to see her as a royal. She suddenly looked back and saw him. She gave a little wave.

Xavier inclined his head in acknowledgement. A moment later she was gone, Bonnet on her heels.

Xavier reached for his phone, dialed a long distance number. When a voice answered, he said, "It's LeDuc. I need to speak to the Prince."

CHAPTER TWO

AMANDA SAT OUTSIDE in the cool morning air. Spring bloomed around her, vibrant colors spilling from trellis boxes and potted planters up and down the street. She enjoyed this spot high on the hill with its view of the ocean. She enjoyed sitting in the fresh air.

And still she fiddled with the ruffled cuff of her sweater dress. Darn Michelle for making her self-conscious of her wardrobe choice. The soft gray mini dress with three rows of ruffles at the hem, paired with black high heeled boots and a flowing purple muffler was the perfect look for an idle Sunday morning.

So maybe it wasn't her clothes choice making her nervous at all. Maybe it was the fact her hot date was late.

Not that Michelle was off the hook. Amanda went through five outfits before deciding on the gray dress. Nothing had felt right. And that wasn't like her, neither the indecisiveness nor the fussiness. She had a long, lean frame that clothes loved, and a sense of style drilled into her by a grandmother obsessed with decorum and good taste.

"Amanda." The deep voice made her name a caress. She looked up and there stood Xavier silhouetted against the morning sun, his shoulders broad beams in an expensive suit.

"Xavier," she breathed. *Oh get a grip, girl. No man respects a pushover.*

"Good morning." He reached for her hand, bent over it before taking his seat.

It was Old World gestures like that that got to her. *He* got to her—his somberness offset by an edgy dangerousness. She had no doubt he was very good at his job.

But she prided herself on being mature, so it was time to act like it.

"Please forgive my tardiness. A last-minute call from home."

"I understand. It must be hard to be away for months at a time."

"Yes." He waved over a waitress, ordered coffee and a Danish. "However, I am a soldier. And it is a prestigious assignment. I am honored to serve my country."

"A soldier?" she asked. "I thought you were a security officer."

"I am an officer of the *Garde royale à la Couronne*. As were my father and his father before him and so on, for six generations."

"A personal guard to the crown—impressive. The exhibit is lovely." She gestured to the newspaper she'd brought with her. "The preview is a great success. You must be proud to be trusted with your country's treasures. Your Prince must have great faith in you."

He was silent for a moment and she worried she might have insulted him. But then he leaned forward as he reached for her hand and played with her fingers.

"That is exactly so. Though many people have felt that it was a lowly assignment."

"I can't see you ever being given a lowly assignment."

He smiled, this time with both his eyes and mouth. She felt he'd given her a special gift.

"A soldier does both the big and the small, because it is all necessary to complete the mission. Of all the generations in my family, I made Commandant at the youngest age."

"And that's an accomplishment?" she asked, though she could see it was.

"Yes. My father is proud of me, my grandfather a little upset."

She laughed and pointed at him. "And you are happy with both reactions."

He shrugged, but a small smile curved the corner of his mouth. "For six generations a son in my father's line has joined the Republican Guard. My family is proud of the exemplary service they have provided to the crown. It is important I demonstrate great skills to honor the Prince's faith in me, and my family before me."

"Wow. But no pressure, right?" He spoke with pride, but there was something, an underlying tension she picked up on that made her wonder if there was more to his story. It prompted her to ask, "What would you do if you weren't a soldier?"

His expression went blank. She actually felt the question stunned him. He shrugged. "An engineer, perhaps, because I have always liked knowing how things work. However, there was never any question of this. It is my duty and my privilege to serve the Prince." He inclined his head again. "But I am a boring topic. We shall speak of you now. What is it you do, Amanda Carn?"

"I'm the assistant curator for the Children's Museum of Art and Science." She lifted her orange juice. "I just celebrated my first year anniversary."

"Congratulations." He touched his mug to her glass.

"A royal guard!" She exclaimed as a thought came to her. "That's perfect. We're doing career presentations at the museum all this month. Would you be willing to come and talk to the kids?"

He considered her for a moment. "When do you have these talks?"

"Tuesdays at four in the afternoon. Please say you'll think about it."

"I will look at my schedule." He promised. "So you like children. Do you have any of your own?"

"No. But I'm an honorary aunt." It thrilled her to say so. "Michelle, you met her last night, is marrying a man who has a child."

"She is brave to take on a ready-made family."

"Funny, I think she's lucky." And he'd hit on another of her fantasies, a big happy family. "I can tell you she's very much in love."

"Then she is, indeed, lucky." He said it simply, sincerely. She liked that he didn't jeer.

"Do you have children?" Turnabout was fair play.

"No. I have never been married."

An interesting response. Was he just sharing information, or were children and marriage linked in his mind? "Do you feel one is a pre-requisite for the other?"

"In my family it always has been. Plus, Pasadonia is a small country. We are not as progressive as the United States."

"Not everyone here is open-minded. I was raised by my grandparents. They're not very progressive at all."

"I understand. My mother would be disappointed in me if I did not treat a woman with respect in all things."

"She sounds like a strong woman." Amanda worked hard to keep the wistfulness from her voice. Her biggest regret in life was never knowing her mother. Her parents.

"She is tough. But she has a huge heart. She is the soul of our family." He set his empty mug on the table. "Why were you raised by your grandparents?"

"They're all the family I have. My mother died when I was just a baby."

He watched her intently, his honey brown eyes focused completely on her. "I am sorry. You must miss her every day."

She nodded, a lump forming in her throat at his simple understanding. Even though she'd never known her mother, Amanda did miss her every day.

"And what of your father? You have not mentioned him."

She sighed. She hadn't known him either, and yes she felt the hole he left in her life, but he was such a mystery that's all she usually focused on. Except for those bitter, lonely minutes when she speculated he must be dead, too. Otherwise why wasn't she with him? Why didn't he come for her?

Xavier leaned forward, his interest apparent. And heady. Especially after the university boys she was used to.

Pleased by his undivided attention, she revealed more than she normally might.

"I don't know my father," she declared. "My mother never told my grandparents who he was."

"How difficult for you. I cannot imagine not knowing one of my parents. Have you made any effort to find him?"

Xavier felt like a thief stealing an innocent woman's secrets. He was a soldier, dammit, not a spy. He did not care for the subterfuge required for this assignment. He already knew the answer to all the questions he'd asked. He'd had a complete dossier of her in his hands before the exhibit ended last night.

After he sent the picture of Amanda to his Prince, His Highness admitted he'd met and wooed an American or two in his early twenties. The Prince also had a copy of the dossier and had viewed a picture of Haley Carn, Amanda's mother. He admitted she looked familiar but could not state with certainty that he knew her twenty-six years ago.

He requested Xavier obtain and forward a DNA sample to Pasadonia. In the meantime he was to maintain surveillance and gather more information.

It was the thing of nightmares.

She shook her head in answer to his question. "I've thought of looking for him, but it always upset my grandmother so much when I asked that I stopped probing."

"So your choice is to give up your search or cause your grandmother distress."

Perhaps if she were a different person he'd find it easier. But he liked her. He found her refreshing, honest, giving, surprisingly bold. And loyal. She'd given up a personal quest to soothe the sensibilities of her grandmother.

"There was no reason to upset her over something I may never know the truth of. But now I'm out on my own, I may try to find out something more."

"Do you have a clue where to look?"

He disliked deceiving her. His gaze landed on her full lips. Especially when he'd prefer to spend time with her for an entirely different reason.

Duty demanded his cooperation, so he would do as his Prince, his friend, requested. It was Xavier's hope that he would quickly be able to prove that her resemblance to the royal family was simply a coincidence.

And then they could move on. She'd be none the wiser, and he'd spend the remainder of his time in this country pleasantly occupied in getting to know her better.

"I think I might. When I was getting ready to move, I took some stuff up to the attic to store. I started to poke around a little, and I found a box with some of my mother's old diaries and journals."

"Sounds promising. Do you think she put your father's name in one of the journals?" That might answer the question for them all. But of course, the Prince would need the DNA proof as well.

"I doubt it. My grandmother would have looked. Unless

she's lied to me all these years, which isn't totally impossible. She's very protective of my mother's memory."

"But not of you?" He found it odd that the dead should take precedence over the living. Yes, we honored and missed those who went ahead of us, but not at the expense of those still with us. Or so he'd been taught.

Amanda dipped her head and played with a spot of water on the table. "My mother was her only child. I'm the one who stole her from my grandparents." She lifted her gaze to his and he saw a world of loneliness in the depths of her sky blue eyes. "It's not that they don't love me on an intellectual level, it's that they can't allow themselves to feel so strongly again. They aren't emotional people."

"Ah." He nodded. "Some people are this way. My family is very emotional."

"That must be nice." Her eyes lit up. He was happy to chase the shadows away. "Do you have a large family?"

"Yes. There is mama and papa and my younger sister, and her entire brood of children. Plus lots of aunts, uncles, cousins."

"It sounds wonderful."

"Yes. And sometimes quite loud."

"Wonderful," she repeated. "So Uncle Xavier. Tell me about your nieces and nephews."

"What is there to tell? There is one of each. Jon is the youngest at one. And Bridgett is four."

"Ah ah." She shook her finger at him. "You pretend disinterest but it's obvious you dote on them. Especially the youngest, Jon."

"Yes." How did she know he had a special affection for Jon, who had his grandfather's naughty grin? "I have missed them."

"But no wife or children for you." She sent him an arch glance. "Are you a player, Xavier?"

"I have no time for games in my life. And too much respect for my mother." As soon as the words left his mouth, he knew Yvette LeDuc would be disappointed in his behavior, even though he acted in the line of duty.

Enough. Except for one last task, he had done all he could for now, all he was willing to do. He deliberately glanced at his watch.

"I must go." He stood and she rose with him. As he hoped she would. He tossed money down to cover their meal and took her hand to lead her to the walkway out front.

She'd worn her lustrous mane of red gold hair free around her shoulders.

"I enjoyed this." She smiled up at him, all innocent charm.

"As did I." He leaned in to kiss her cheek, lifting his hand to her hair, feeling like a beast as he did so. The silkiness wrapped around his wrist, catching in his watch. "Will you have dinner with me tonight?"

She hesitated long enough for him to remember she'd issued this invitation for coffee at her friend's prompting. Finally she nodded.

"Yes. Ouch!" She reached for her hair when he began to lower his hand.

"My apologies." He stopped and carefully extracted his hand, taking care not to pull her hair once he'd caught a few strands in his watch. "Such lovely hair. And now I have a memento of our morning together."

"Amanda, please carry the tray of dressed olives," Ingrid Carn directed from the other side of the counter. Statuesque in a tailored navy pantsuit, her silver hair short and stylish, she was a striking woman. "I'm so pleased you could make it this evening. We haven't seen you in ages."

"I came for Sunday dinner last weekend," Amanda reminded her grandmother.

Doing as directed, she picked up the tray and followed the older woman from the stainless steel and granite kitchen to the parlor where light walls and fabrics offset dark wood and heavy furniture. There was nothing dainty about Ingrid Carn.

"I do hope we'll see you more than the occasional weekend," Grandmother said tightly. "Your grandfather misses you. Posture, dear."

Automatically Amanda straightened her shoulders as she sat. Always it was her grandfather's emotions at risk, never her grandmother's—an obvious detachment ploy, and to this day it hurt every time she did it.

Especially tonight, since Amanda had given up her date with Xavier to attend her grandmother's little fête. Not that having a little extra time to consider her decision to see him again was a bad thing. She enjoyed her time with him, perhaps too much. His confidence, the way he listened, his dangerous air of alertness contradicted by his love of family made him fascinating—just as his accent and Old World courtesies made him charming.

A lethal combination for an unsophisticated girl.

What could he possibly see in her?

This is where Michelle would remind Amanda he was only in town long enough to have a good time. That left her with a good news, bad news scenario. The good news was he'd only be here for six weeks so she didn't have to worry about trust and commitment issues. But what if she really fell for him? The bad news was he'd only be here for a few weeks.

So when Grandmother called this afternoon and demanded Amanda drop everything and join them for a small reception Ingrid was hosting for the Dean of Historical Studies, Amanda accepted in the hope that a little extra time would bring resolution to her internal struggle.

"I'm still getting settled into my new place." Amanda made

the same excuse she'd been using for six months. "Plus it's a long trip for the middle of the week."

Which explained why Amanda chose the apartment she did. She loved her grandparents but she craved freedom. Living too close to them would negate the independence she achieved by moving out of their home.

"Yes, I know how distressed you were to move so far away." Ingrid settled on the couch beside Amanda. "That's why I've invited the Dean here tonight. They're looking for an assistant to catalog and digitize the History Library."

Amanda's heart sank into her stomach. This was an elaborate job interview instigated by her grandmother to get Amanda back in her domain.

No. Please no.

Amanda had spent her whole life under her grandmother's thumb, subject to her strict standards, always conscious of the stringent scrutiny of being related to not one but two senior professors of the university. Always aware her behavior reflected on them as well as herself. It was a burden she felt acutely.

She'd just gained her freedom, and was revelling in the autonomy of big city life. She loved her little apartment and she wasn't giving it up now she'd had a taste of liberty.

"Grandmother," she said gently, because she may be resolute, but she didn't want to hurt the other woman. "I'm very happy at the children's museum."

"I know dear, but this is a wonderful opportunity. You'd be able to move back here."

"But I like my apartment. I like my job. We've talked about this. I'm twenty-five years old. It's time for me to leave the nest."

"This is a very prestigious position. I thought of you as soon as I heard about it."

"Because it's close to home. not because I'm suited to the position."

She huffed. "You love to read."

"Yes, and I enjoy a good library, but I don't want to work in one."

"Now, you're just being difficult."

"I'm not. I love you, and these were hard choices to make, but they were the right choices for me."

"You're too young," Grandmother snapped. "I've said it all along, just as I said your mother was too young for that trip. I was right then, and I'm right now."

"My mother?" The reference threw Amanda. Grandmother rarely spoke of Haley. Though she'd been on Amanda's mind a lot after talking with Xavier yesterday and being reminded of the box she'd found with the old diaries.

Xavier had assumed Amanda had them, but she didn't. Excited by the discovery, she'd asked Grandmother if she could take the box with her. Grandmother had said no, and had refused to discuss the matter further.

"What trip?" Amanda asked her grandmother.

"That year before she had you, some college friends of hers were going on a post-graduation trip to Europe. She had a bee in her bonnet about going with them. I was against it from the beginning. She was too young, too naïve. They all were."

"Life brings experience." It was one of her grandfather's favorite sayings.

Grandmother closed her eyes. "That's what she said. How could we argue with our own beliefs?"

"You let her go."

"Yes. And she came back pregnant with you."

Amanda flinched at the venom in the words. She knew her grandmother's feelings about her mother's pregnancy. She knew she was blamed for her mother's death.

She lived knowing her grandparents would choose her mother over her every time. She understood. And at the same time she didn't. Haley was their child. But Amanda was here. Why couldn't they just love her? Isn't that what Haley would have wanted?

Accepting the futility of fighting what couldn't be changed, she pushed the ache aside and focused on what grandmother revealed about Haley. Maybe Amanda would learn something about her father after all.

"So she met my father in Europe?" How funny to hear this now, when Xavier had just been asking if she had any relations in Pasadonia.

"Yes." Grandmother stood to straighten the glasses on the bar, to arrange the wine, open and breathing, precisely next to the bottle of Bourbon. "We never met the man who stole our baby from us."

"Did she tell you anything about him?" Amanda asked softly, afraid to disturb the moment.

"They flew into England, made it their base. She called often to tell us all about their little jaunts. She did not mention meeting a man. I would have remembered."

"Yes. So my father is English."

"Possibly. She was gone for two months. They started out in England but bounced around from there. They also went to Ireland, Paris, Milan, Pasadonia."

"My mother was in Pasadonia twenty-five years ago?" How was that for coincidence?

"Yes. They spent at least a week there." Grandmother moved back to the sofa, rearranged the trays on the coffee table. "I don't care to speak of that time."

"Of course, I understand," Amanda said, like she always did. But suddenly it wasn't true. At what point did her feelings matter? Obviously never, if she didn't push the issue. "I know it upsets you to talk about Haley. But I long to know her better. I didn't even know she'd been on this trip, or that my father was European."

"You don't need to know anything about him except that he stole our child from us."

"That's not good enough anymore. I have questions. Who was he? Why didn't she tell you anything about him? Did he know about me?"

"Do not take that tone with me, young lady." Grandmother chastised her in icy tones. "I've said I don't care to talk about it."

"Then let me read her journals," she said reasonably. "I can get my answers from them."

"I said no."

"Why not?" Amanda worked hard to keep the pleading from her voice. Grandmother would latch onto any sign of weakness.

"They're private." She stated stiffly.

"She's dead, Grandmother." Amanda made it a gentle reminder. "I think she'd want me to have them."

"It's out of the question."

The no give attitude finally spiked Amanda's temper.

"Now who's being stubborn?" she demanded. "You won't tell me about her, but I can't read the journals. She's my mother! Would you have wanted her to have no knowledge of you? Can't you understand that my knowing her doesn't take anything away from you?"

When there was no answer, Amanda shook her head sadly. "Enjoy your dinner. I'm afraid I can't stay." She walked to the closet for her coat and purse.

"Don't you dare leave," Grandmother snapped. "My guests are expecting to meet you."

"Regarding a job I don't want." Amanda's stomach roiled

and her voice shook, but she stood up to her grandmother. Stood up for herself. "Just tell them I didn't care to talk about it. That always works for you."

CHAPTER THREE

"THIS IS AMAZING." Amanda stopped next to Xavier. They stood in front of the glass display of the royal crown of Pasadonia. She whispered, otherwise her voice echoed through the cavernous room.

After dinner, he'd brought her here to the museum for a personal after hours tour of the crown jewels. They were alone except for the night security—two guards who stood at opposite ends of the vast room.

She'd like to think her decision to keep their date came from carefully considered deliberation, but the truth was he drew her more than anyone she'd ever met. And it gave her great pleasure knowing Grandmother would heartily disapprove.

It may be petty, but Amanda didn't care.

And she was having a really good time.

"The jewels are stunning." Hands behind her back, she leaned forward to study the three crowns on display. "The workmanship is exquisite."

"Only the highest quality gems are used in the making of the royal crowns. Pasadonia uses the same jeweller and silversmith as the Royal house of Britain. There are over two thousand precious gems in the coronation crown, known as the St. Martin."

"St. Martin of Tours, patron saint of soldiers." She strolled

on to a display of scepters. At his questioning look she confessed, "I did a Google search."

"Yes. We are a small country but we have held our own
through the centuries."

"Le Valliant allié." She read on the shaft of a gleaming
gold scepter. "The valiant ally."

"Our motto, and a way of life. We believe in making
friends not enemies."

"A nice sentiment," she nodded and moved on to a cabinet
of daggers, the decorative knives were as beautiful as they
were lethal. "But in my experience politics aren't that easy.
It's not always possible to be everyone's friend."

"Perhaps not, but when you control a neutral port in the
Gulf of Lions, it is possible to avoid making enemies."

"I would think that would make you all the more vulner-
able to invasion."

He inclined his dark head. "As I said, we are small but we
held our own. Pasadonia has always had a strong militia. We
are fierce fighters."

"To this day?" she asked curiously. Looking at his profile
she saw the pride in him, and when he turned his golden gaze
her way, she saw the fierceness he spoke of.

So why had she sensed an underlying tension when he'd
talked of his family's history in the royal guard?

"Yes," he said simply. "Pasadonia has all the problems of
any nation in these days of unrest. Terrorism is a universal
issue. Our Prince is a vocal member of the International Security Consortium. Our militia must be ever vigilant."

"Of course." How small-minded of her not to associate big
world problems with a small principality.

"We protect our Prince. We protect our borders. We protect
and aid our citizens." He gestured to the elaborate exhibit.
"We protect our national resources. We stand in the middle
of Pasadonia right now. These are my country's treasures.

They are my responsibility. I will protect them with my life as I would if we were in my homeland."

"I can see you're very dedicated." She placed her hand on his, where it rested on the corner of a display case. "Your country has beautiful treasures. Considering the uncertain times, I'm actually surprised your Prince would send the jewels on tour."

"Tourism is a large part of our economy. With people traveling less these days, our economy was suffering. The tour has generated a large influx of necessary income."

"Your Prince is smart to use the riches of your history to finance your current and future needs. From what I've read the tour has been incredibly successful."

"It has. My Prince is very pleased with the generosity of your country and its citizens."

She laughed. "Americans are fascinated by all things royal. Probably because it's not something we've ever known."

The next turn took them by the tiaras. Diamonds, sapphires, emeralds and rubies looped and swooped in delicate designs, layering gem upon gem so it glittered like fallen stars.

"Oh." Again she clasped her hands behind her back, an old habit to keep from reaching for something she shouldn't touch.

He tugged on her fingers. "I am sorry I cannot let you handle the jewels."

She grinned at him. "I'd love that, but I understand. I used to dream of being a princess when I was little. All little girls do." She glanced at the brilliant display, sighed. "I never imagined anything this elaborate. This beautiful."

"Ah, so you are all grown up now? There are no more dreams of tiaras, ballgowns, or finding prince charming?" His expression remained somber, but the words teased.

"Not for a long time. Not for me anyway." She looked at

him, and then away, while heat flowed into her cheeks as she confessed, "My favorite play time princess was Rapunzel until one day I realized I related to her because I also felt trapped."

"Amanda." He immediately took her elbow, turned her to face him. "Has someone hurt you?"

His intensity made it clear he was ready to do something about it if someone had.

She shook her head, gently touched his cheek in gratitude for his concern. "No. But my upbringing was very strict. My grandparents are very traditional."

"And they lost their child."

"Yes." She nodded grateful for his understanding. "So they were doubly cautious with me. And we practically lived on the campus of the university. They always made it clear my actions reflected on their reputations. Rapunzel grew up in a hidden tower. I grew up in an ivory tower."

Hearing the bitterness in her voice, she lifted a shoulder and let it drop in a nonchalant gesture. "It's fanciful I know. Sorry. I don't mean to drop this on you. I'm probably not even making sense."

"Ivory tower, I know what this term means." He tucked the fall of her hair behind her shoulder, ran his hand down the back of her arm until he reached her hand and laced their fingers together. "You felt restricted by the inhibiting milieu of your grandparents' world."

"That's it exactly." He was so insightful, so easy to talk to. Though why she was sharing this with him, she couldn't say. They were feelings she barely acknowledged to herself, but apparently her recent argument with grandmother had allowed stifled emotions to rise to the surface. Perhaps she felt safe with Xavier because their relationship was so finite.

"The six months since I moved into my own apartment have been wonderful."

"How have your grandparents taken your departure?"

She bit her lip. "I thought they had accepted it, but the dinner I went to the other night was a bid to get me back into their sphere. The History Department is looking for an assistant to catalog and digitize the history library."

"A prestigious position, I'm sure."

The corner of her mouth twitched up. "That's what Grandmother said." Which reminded Amanda of what else Grandmother had revealed. Amanda gestured to the tiara. "This is the crown Princess Vivienne is wearing in the portrait, isn't it?"

"Yes." He led her to the painting of Vivienne. "It was made for her for the Coronation of her husband Prince Louis II in 1852."

Amanda thought about telling him about her mother's trip to Europe, to Pasadonia, but hesitated. What if he thought she was trying to claim some type of kinship with the Prince?

She didn't want their budding relationship—wait, relationship was too strong a word—their budding *friendship* to be cut short because she made too much of a simple coincidence.

No, she chided herself, she was being silly. Her resemblance to Princess Vivienne wasn't that strong.

"So guess what?" She wandered a few steps away, pretended an interest in a display she didn't really see. "I found out my mother took a trip to Europe the summer before I was born. She went with some friends after college. Traveled to several different countries, including Pasadonia."

He west still, then very deliberately advanced on her. "How interesting." He trailed a finger down her cheek. "Perhaps there is a relationship to the Princess. Should I address you as Your Highness?"

She graced him with a teasing smile. "Do I get to wear the tiara?"

"Hmm." He arched a brow as if contemplating her question. "Ah, no."

"Spoilsport."

"All part of the job." He shrugged. "Unless you want to take a DNA test and—"

"Okay, okay." She glanced at her watch. Time had flown—it was already an hour later than she'd meant to stay out tonight. Time to go.

"Thanks for the private tour. I've really enjoyed learning more about your country." And him. "But it's getting late and I have to be up early."

"Of course." He bowed his acceptance. "I will walk you to your car."

"Oh, that's not necessary. My car is just across the street," She protested. "You finish up what you have to do here."

"It is necessary. I would do this for any woman. But for you it is also my pleasure."

Charmed, she accepted his offer, happy to have a few more minutes of his company.

Outside, the fog hung heavy in the air, reducing visibility and dampening sound. It gave Amanda the sense that she and Xavier were alone in a mystic world. She laughed silently. She may not romanticize princesses any more, but fantasy still lingered.

She shivered and was rewarded with the warm weight of Xavier's hand in the small of her back. A moment ago she'd bragged that her car was nearby. Now they seemed to reach her little red Civic way too soon.

He took her keys, unlocked and opened the door, and bent to check the interior. He was most thorough in seeing to her safety. The effort gave her a warm feeling. It was probably habit for him, but the extra care made her feel cherished.

"Thank you." She lifted her eyes to his. Would he kiss her? She wanted him to kiss her.

He held up her keys and she opened her hand. He placed the keys in her palm, curled her fingers around them. All without taking his eyes from hers.

He had her ensnared, captivated. Wanting more.

Should she kiss him? Why not? She was a modern woman, confident, sexy. Even with the pep talk she wasn't that brave. He just wasn't the kind of man you made moves on.

Though the latent heat in his eyes told her the advances wouldn't be unwelcome, he made no move of his own. Maybe mention of her mother's trip to Pasadonia had changed the dynamics between them.

"Well, good night."

Friendship, she reminded herself, and tore her gaze away from his. She moved to stand in the open door. Then stopped because he refused to release her hand. Surprised, she looked back. At full smolder, he slowly reeled her toward him.

Now the moment was here, her heart fluttered wildly, her blood dancing as his head lowered to hers. She sighed and melted against him. Yes.

His lips settled softly on hers. At the touch of his tongue she opened to him, sighing as she drank in the taste of him.

All thoughts of friendship flittered away into the night. This was no friendly peck. This kiss sizzled her senses, titillated everything female in her.

It took only a moment for her to realize she'd only ever known boys before this. Xavier was all man. He knew what he wanted and took it.

And she gave, leaping into the embrace with wonder and enthusiasm. Arms locked around his neck, she reveled in his strength, in the feel of his hands on her. Her toes actually curled as she sought purchase for her shaky legs.

A car passed them on the opposite side of the street. The intrusion of reality into their world caused Xavier to lift his head. Gently he feathered kisses across her cheek and whispered sexy words in her ear.

"*Tu me fais oublier moi-même*. You make me forget myself."

"Me too." Necking on the street? Her grandmother would freak. But Amanda couldn't bring herself to care. All she could think of was more.

"I must say goodnight." With obvious reluctance, he saw her safely seated. And then he stepped back and raised his hand in farewell.

She pressed her hand to the window and made herself drive away. She blew out a breath that lifted the bangs off her forehead. Oh boy. She was so lost. Absolutely gone. He made her feel alive, feminine, desirable.

She knew she was setting herself up for heartbreak. He'd be leaving in a few weeks and her life was here. There was no future to this relationship.

But better heartache than regret. She was tired of being afraid to trust. Tired of letting fear rule her. She felt safe with Xavier. And she longed to explore the chemistry that sizzled between them. She didn't want to look back and wish she'd had the courage to grab life and live it to the fullest for the time they had together.

She was going into it with her eyes open. But oh yeah, she was going for it.

Xavier strolled back to the museum, his gaze locked on the vehicle carrying Amanda Carn into the night. When the car turned from his sight, he fixed his gaze forward and tried to calculate exactly how big a mistake he'd just made.

For the first time, man and soldier were at odds as desire warred with duty. He liked this woman, he wanted her physically, but if she was of the royal family, his duty was to protect her against all threats, including himself. With the addictive taste of her still on his lips, he recognized the challenge that represented.

Inside he did a final walk through of the entire museum, as was his habit, ending with the exhibit rooms.

He knew his duty, lived and breathed it day in and day out. Duty was what kept the soldier from kissing her when she so obviously wanted a kiss as much as he wanted to get his mouth on her. The shadow of hurt as she moved away drew the man in him forward as he sought to erase her pain.

And his.

Now may be the only time he had with her, this time of uncertainty while the DNA test was pending. Once her identity was confirmed, she'd be forever out of his reach. And after seeing her next to Vivienne's portrait again tonight and hearing her mother had been in Pasadonia, he had little doubt a royal connection would be made.

Satisfied the facility was secure he gave his men final instructions and signed out at the security desk.

"Did your date enjoy the private show?" the duty officer asked congenially.

"Yes," Xavier answered evenly. "She works for one of the local museums so she appreciated the value of the collection."

"Huh," the guard made a disappointed noise. "She looks a lot like one of the portraits. I thought she might be visiting royalty."

"No," Xavier denied firmly. "She's just a beautiful woman and a friend."

That was his answer. Until notified otherwise, Amanda was just an attractive woman he wanted to get to know better. The soldier's orders were to keep her close, to obtain information.

The man intended to do just that.

CHAPTER FOUR

AMANDA LET HERSELF into her apartment still floating high on that goodnight kiss. She'd replayed the date over and over in her head, reliving the best night of her life.

Dinner at The Top of the Mark proved a feast for the soul. Thirty-four floors in the sky, the revolving restaurant provided a panoramic view of the city. She felt like she was eating among the stars, making the four-course meal a gourmet dream.

And that wasn't even the best part. Xavier elevated the experience to a whole new level. Attentive and charming, the conversation flowed so smoothly time flew.

She kicked off her shoes and set them neatly in the closet as she remembered the trip to the museum where he gave her a personal tour of the exhibit he protected so zealously.

The jewels and costumes took on extra meaning as he spoke of the events, both violent and celebratory, where they'd been worn or used. Coronations, balls, and battles—the entire collection represented a way of life far beyond her imagining. It seemed the thing of fairy tales, but grittier, with all the trials and tribulations of real life, of real people.

And his kiss. Oh my.

He made her feel as if she'd never been kissed before. And she hadn't, not by a man of his experience. And yet it wasn't practiced. It was totally personal, totally focused, totally intense.

He'd made her toes curl, her skin tingle and her body shiver in the best possible way. With longing and need.

Stripping in the bathroom, she placed her dress in the dry cleaning, her lingerie in the hamper.

She'd never needed before. Not that her experience was vast. Sure she'd kissed a few guys, but she'd only had one lover, and it had been pleasant enough, but it turned out he was more interested in a good grade from her grandmother than in Amanda.

Big mistake on both their parts.

In the shower she admitted this thing with Xavier may be a mistake as well. She'd let anger at her grandmother propel her into a date she was leery of. And already it would hurt more to walk away from him than it had to leave the jerk who was only after academic acclaim. She missed being with Xavier, wanted to call and see if he made it back to the hotel okay, if they were taking good care of him, if he liked her as much as she liked him.

Her lack of experience rose up in a tide of insecurity as she wondered if he found her immature. She hoped not. Couldn't believe he did. Those kisses were in no way juvenile.

Enough already. Any more rehashing and she'd revert to grade school mentality and sock him in the arm the next time she saw him. She needed something to occupy her mind or she'd never get to sleep tonight.

A knock sounded at the door. She frowned, unaccustomed to getting company so late. A glance through the peephole showed her manager. She opened the door.

"Amanda. You had a delivery today. I heard you come in so I thought I'd bring it up."

"Thanks, Mr. Vey." She took the box and bid the man good night.

Recognizing the box that contained her mother's diaries, Amanda carried it to her bed and opened it. Inside she found a note from Grandmother.

Amanda,
Your grandfather believes your disappointing behavior the other night was the result of distress. You can thank him for this.
Grandmother.

Even as she read the note, Amanda didn't know if she could believe it or not. Was this another example of Grandmother ascribing her own feelings to Grandfather, or had he really put his foot down?

Eager to get to the journals, she decided to brood on the issue at another time. Instead she started pulling out books. She pulled one out and flipped to the first page. And found the first reference to her father.

I never believed in love at first sight until I met him, my prince. I know, it's childish. But that's how he makes me feel, as if I've found my Prince Charming. Maybe it's because I'm in Europe where castles abound and royalty is a reality.

I know I can't trust the feeling. I hear mother's voice in my head cataloging all the reasons why I should keep my distance, but I can't. I won't.

I can't stop thinking about him. He makes me happy. And we haven't even been alone; always we've been in a crowd of friends though we've spent hours talking. And today he stole a kiss.

Stole? Why do I say that when I wanted it so badly? And he actually made my toes curl. I'll never look on that term as a cliché again.

Amanda laughed, relating with her mother as she read on.

The next time he asks me out I'm going to agree. It may be foolish to pursue a relationship when I'm here for such a short time. Mother would say so. But feelings this strong deserve a chance. If I know it's not for forever then I should be safe, right?

I haven't journaled for years but I needed to put my thoughts in order, and this helped. Maybe it will help, too, to read about my romantic adventure when summer is over and I'm back home in the position mother has chosen for me. Or since I'm being brave here, it'll give me courage to be brave there and seek a position of my own choosing.

Amanda read the next two entries but her mother's "prince" had had to pop away on business and it was mostly angst about her original decision not to go out with him, and how she wouldn't make that mistake again if she did, please God, get to see him again, and he still wanted to see her alone.

A lesson learned to grab opportunity when it hammered on your door.

Closing the book, Amanda checked her alarm and then switched out the light. Thank goodness for Michelle, and the push she gave Amanda at the preview event. Otherwise she'd be like her mother, wishing and regretting what might have been instead of remembering a fabulous kiss.

With a sigh she closed her eyes and let her mind take her back to Xavier's embrace.

Xavier wore his dress uniform for his talk at the museum. His role as senior security officer for the exhibition called for discretion so he and his men wore black suits with white

shirts and a black tie adorned by a tie pin of the Royal Republican Guard crest.

But for this event the he figured if he was speaking on
being a royal guard he should look like one. The pants were
navy with a gold-banded red stripe down the outside of the
leg; the jacket was stark white with black epaulettes and red
braiding looped over the right shoulder. Medals and ribbons
earned through the course of duty decorated his chest to the
left.

At home he'd wear his dress sword sheathed at his side. As
this was a peace mission, he'd left it locked up in his quarters
at home. In its place he'd borrowed one of the simpler weapons from the collection and carried it in a long leather case.

The Children's Museum of Art and Science sat on the
edge of Golden Gate Park. A two story red brick and tow-
ering glass building, it married the romance of art and the
clarity of science.

Inside, a woman seated at the information desk directed
him up a flight of stairs and to the left.

"Oh the kids are going to love you." She chortled. "I might
sneak up and have a peak myself."

He thanked her and bowed, earning another trill of delight. The corner of his mouth curled up as he took the stairs.
American women were so easy to charm.

He found Amanda surrounded by children ranging in ages
from about six to ten. She sat in their midst holding a copy
of the *Little Engine That Could,* explaining the mechanics
of a steam engine.

The kids were totally into the lesson. And it quickly became clear they were trying to trip her up. But she stayed on
point and answered all their questions, patient and in control.

"Why do they call it a choo-choo train?" One youngster
asked.

Amanda reached down and picked up a large picture of a

steam engine. "Well, see in this diagram how the steam vents out into the air?"

"Yeah," the kids called.

"When this valve opens, the steam escapes in a rush of pressure making a choo-ing sound. As the train starts, this piston," she pointed to the diagram, making sure all the kids could see, "is moving very slowly, but once the train starts rolling the piston gains speed and the exhaust is released faster and faster and each time it goes choo, choo, choo."

"Thoo-thoo train," declared a little boy missing his front teeth.

"That's right." Amanda looked up and spied Xavier.

Her face lit up, showing her delight in seeing him. His gut tightened as an answering pleasure swelled in him.

But he had no time to worry over the warmth of his reaction to her interaction with the kids. She was a natural with them, a clear indication she'd make a good mother someday.

Noticing her attention had strayed, the children followed her gaze to him.

"It's Prince Charming." A little girl gasped.

Mon dieu. The Lord save him. He supposed he did look a bit like the cartoon character in his uniform. The Lord knew he never wanted the pressure that came with the crown.

Duty and friendship put him close enough to the Prince to see what he dealt with on a daily bases. The demands—everyone wanted something from him—the politics, the economy, the public appearances…it was never ending, and it all fell on the Prince's shoulders.

"He does look as handsome as Prince Charming, doesn't he?" Amanda saved him. "But Prince Charming is a character in a book. This is Xavier Marcel LeDuc, Commandant of the Royal Pasadonian Republican Guard. He's a real Royal Guard to the Prince of Pasadonia."

"Wow." The exclamation came in one voice.

Xavier bit back a grin and bowed to his audience. The little girl who called him Prince Charming melted to her knees. He met Amanda's gaze and she winked at him. That did win a smile.

"It is my pleasure to meet you," he said to the small crowd of children. "Miss Carn has kindly asked me here to talk to you about my profession."

"Yes." Amanda took control. "Everyone take a seat. We'll let Commandant LeDuc speak for a few minutes and then you can ask some questions."

Taking his hand, she led him to the front of the group then she squeezed his hand and left him to it.

"Wait. Hold this." He pushed the leather carrying case into Amanda's hands.

She gasped a little at the weight. "What is it?"

"Visual aid. I borrowed a sword from the collection, but I did not realize it would be such young children."

"Oh my, that would be an impressive show and tell." She bit her lip as if considering the idea and then shook her head.

"You're right, they're too young. They'd want to touch." She grinned. "You can show me later."

He deliberately put the thought of showing her his sword from his mind as he turned to his task. Looking at the young faces he realized he needed to keep this simple.

"Pasadonia is a small country in Europe, and instead of a president we have a Prince. This lovely young lady called me Prince Charming, but in fact I'm the person who guards the Prince."

"Like the secret serve guys?" One of the older boys asked. "I saw them in a movie."

"Yes, the Secret Service is an agency responsible for protecting the President and other important dignitaries. I am a soldier. In Pasadonia there are two branches of the military, one is civil defense and the other is responsible for protecting the royal family."

"If you're a soldier, how come you don't have any weapons?" a husky kid with spiked blond hair and freckles demanded. "The policeman who talked to us had a gun."

"Unlike law enforcement, soldiers only carry weapons when there is a need to do so."

"What kind of weapons do you use?"

"When I guard the Prince, I carry a nine millimeter Glock. We are also trained to defend and fight against a knife attack."

"What about a sword?" a girl chirped. "Prince Charming has a sword."

His glance slid to the four-foot-long case Amanda held against her front as if hugging a part of him to her.

"Swords are not used in modern warfare, however, Pasadonia is a traditional country. Swords are a formal part of our dress uniforms, and all members of the militia are required to be proficient swordsmen."

"Ohh," the girl sighed.

"Cool!" a boy crowed.

"Swords are sissy." A husky kid scoffed.

Giving the irritating child a hard-eyed smile, Xavier said, "As I stated, they are not used in today's military."

Amanda stepped forward. "Show him the sword."

He lifted an eyebrow. "I don't need to prove myself to a child."

"Of course not," she agreed readily. "Show him anyway. You can step behind the bug counter. The kids will be able to see but won't be able to reach it." She held out the case.

Xavier surveyed the situation. He spoke the truth when he told Amanda he had no need to prove himself to a child, but he did have a drive to please her. Still, the safety of all must be considered. He moved behind the glass cabinet she'd indicated to see if it would suit. It was high enough most of the children had to stand back to see.

Excellent. The kids, with the exception of his heckler, had been well behaved and several adults were stepping closer, showing interest, so it should be fine. He set the leather carrying case on top of the cabinet and unzipped it.

Amanda faced the children. "Commandant DeLuc has brought a sword to show you. This is a very old weapon and it is part of the collection on display at the Art History museum. Stay on this side of the counter. And no touching."

He removed his jacket, handing it to Amanda before pulling out a pair of leather gloves and donning them to handle the weapon. With sure, precise moves, he lifted the scabbard free of the case.

Holding the scabbard straight out in front of him, he grasped the ornate hilt and pulled the sword free. Metal slid over metal with a sweet swish as the engraved sword was revealed.

A hum of approval sounded from the group. He carefully lifted the weapon and held it up for them to see.

"Awesome."

"Look at the pretty jewels."

"Shiny."

"It looks really sharp."

"Is it heavy?"

Finally a question.

"A little," Xavier replied. "Remember this is a weapon and it can be dangerous if mishandled. This particular sword was made for Prince Jean Claude III. Our current Prince is Jean Claude VI."

Setting the scabbard on the glass, he hefted the sword, enjoying the weight, the feel of it in his hand. A champion fencer, the tour had cut into his practice regimen. Handling the sword reminded him how much he missed it, how much he missed the workouts with his father.

He swallowed hard and concentrated on describing the sword instead of the sudden longing for home, for family. The distraction worked, and the moment of weakness passed. Catching Amanda's gaze eased the last of the loneliness.

He addressed the need for safety and demonstrated a few moves, drawing a larger crowd.

It occurred to him the sooner he wrapped this up, the sooner he would have Amanda to himself. A surreptitious glance at his watch confirmed he had met his agreed-upon thirty minutes. He wrapped up with the story of how Prince Jean Claude III used this sword when he led his army of two hundred men against an invasion of Pasadonia in 1848.

"Supporters of Prince Carlos of Spain sought to gain land revenue for his bid to claim the crown by overtaking our valuable port. Jean Claude and his men defeated the larger army. Spain was denied access to the port and our goods for a year at which point Queen Isabel II reinforced her alliance by sending Prince Jean Claude a cache of a hundred guns. But it was a sword that won the assault."

"How big was the other army?" the blond kid asked.

"The odds were nearly two to one."

"And that's all we have time for today." Amanda stepped up and took control. "Please help me in thanking Commandant LeDuc for his wonderful presentation."

A round of applause came from the gathering and several people surged forward with a barrage of questions. Xavier pasted on a smile and answered easily. Though it appeared some would like a closer look at the sword, he calmly and firmly packed it away.

He kept an eye on Amanda who was busy handing children off to their parents and restoring the presentation area to order. When she headed his way, he bowed formally to the last two lingering gentlemen and made his leave of them.

A huge smile on her face, Amanda wrapped him in a hug. "That was fabulous. Thank you so much."

"A response like that almost makes putting up with that little puck worth it."

She grinned and led him toward the exit. "I think you mean little punk."

"This too." He shrugged, nonchalant. "For you it was my pleasure. It felt good to hold a sword again."

"You were very impressive."

"It is a skill all soldiers in Pasadonia must perfect. There are many tournaments. I enjoy competing."

"I bet you win, too."

"I do, yes." He helped her into her coat and whispered in her ear, "I would like to show you what I can do with my sword."

CHAPTER FIVE

AMANDA LAUGHED AND uncharacteristically turned into his arms, looping hers around his neck. Her mother's regret at not grabbing the chance she had to spend time with the man who'd so quickly caught her interest sparked Amanda to act spontaneously.

She braved a kiss, and sighed into his ready response. Then, because they were still too close to the museum, she grabbed his free hand and began walking again.

The fact her mother ended up pregnant and alone was something she chose not to dwell on.

"You're flirting, and I love it." The glance she shot him held a twinge of shyness in spite of her best efforts to appear confident. "But I know a distraction when I hear it. Tell me more about your fencing. And your family. They must be very proud of you."

"Can a parent be too proud?" he asked ruefully. "That would be my mother. She is my biggest fan. My father encourages her, making sure she knows of all my public events."

Amanda cringed for him. "Does she embarrass you?"

"Do I wish she were less verbal, yes. Am I embarrassed, no." He stopped next to his luxury rental car, held the door open for her. "My family is very demonstrative. My sister and I learned early in life that support and love would be lavished on us. If we protested, it became even more exaggerated. Best not to fight it."

"How lovely," she whispered as he rounded the hood of the car. To know such approval, such love. He'd had to fight it off while she pulled apart every sentence her grandparents uttered trying to find one word of praise or affection.

She had a moment of disquiet as she contemplated how different they were. Not only did they come from different worlds, their life experiences were so dissimilar how could they hope to find common ground?

And then he slid into his seat and reached for her hand. He brought her fingers to his mouth for a warm kiss as admiration lit his light brown eyes.

"Where would you like to go for dinner?" he asked, his breath warm against her palm.

When he looked at her like that, when he touched her, all qualms disappeared. Just being together was enough.

"Amanda?" he prompted.

"Oh." What had he asked? Oh yeah, dinner. "Let's go to the wharf and play tourist. In fact, as a reward for coming to help me at the museum today, I want you to pick anywhere or anything you want to do in San Francisco and I will be your personal tour guide, my treat."

"This is not necessary. I am proud to represent my country to the youth of America." He started the engine, flashed her a wry glance before pulling into traffic. "Even the little puck."

"Punk," she corrected. Again.

"This too."

"You're funny. Why do you keep calling him a puck?"

"A puck is a small, round object you would like to knock around, yes?"

"Xavier!" she exclaimed, her tone chiding. "So your mother comes to your fencing tournaments. What about your father?"

"My father also attends the tournaments, but as a competitor. He is the best, and he taught me. I can beat him, but he makes me sweat. He holds many records and he will receive a prestigious award for his accomplishments as well as a commendation in a couple of weeks for his many years of service to the crown at the annual *Hommage aux Forces.*"

"A couple of weeks? So you're going to miss the celebration? That's sad."

"No. I will return to Pasadonia for a week to participate in the festivities." A frown creased his brow. "I will miss you. That is sad."

The news saddened her as well. To distract them both she changed the topic.

"So, what would you like to do? We can do Alcatraz, or stay in San Francisco and do Chinatown, Lombard Street. Or we can skip town and do Napa Valley, the redwoods, or Yosemite."

He squeezed her hand in appreciation. "Since you bring it up, I have always wondered about Alcatraz. But you must have been there many times and would be bored."

"No. I've only been a few times. Plus this is for you. It's a date. On Thursday, it'll be you, me, and The Rock."

My days are now defined by the time spent with JC and the time waiting to see him again. I love our time together, his sense of humor, his kindness, his sense of adventure. He's so smart and mature for his age as his is often the voice of reason in the crowd.

And we're always in a crowd. His friends are so zealous with him you could mistake them for bodyguards. How he laughed when I told him that. And then he stole me away for precious alone time.

I'm not so fond of his control. He's a master at stopping before we go too far. He's so hot, and it feels so good when

I'm in his arms. I want him and it hurts to think he doesn't want me enough to go all the way.

Maybe it has something to do with the sadness I sometimes see in him. He does a good job of hiding it most of the time but there are moments when he grows pensive and I can see it in the grimness of his mouth, the shadow in the back of his eyes.

I know it has to do with his family, but he rarely speaks of them and I hate to pry when his reluctance to share is so clear. Still, I wished I could help more. The best I can do is be there for him and take his mind off whatever upsets him so.

My friends and I have invited the guys on a picnic to celebrate the 4th of July—we obviously miss home more than we let on to each other—and I'm hoping to convince JC to go all the way. I'm ready for some fireworks of my own.

Amanda tucked a red ribbon into her mom's diary to mark her place and set the book on her white wicker nightstand. She understood her mother's joy and her frustration.

Amanda's heart resonated in woman-to-woman kindred-ship when her mother mentioned how JC defined her time. It was as if Haley spoke directly to Amanda in matters of love.

Not that she loved Xavier. She clicked off the bedside light and drew the covers up to her chest.

She was smarter than that, but she couldn't deny the man owned her thoughts. She was either with him or thinking of being with him.

As for the frustration? There were definitely times when Xavier was way too much of a gentleman.

It made her cheeks burn just to admit that. And still she longed for him. They met up most days and yet it wasn't enough.

Tonight he'd had an event so she hadn't seen him today. But tomorrow was Thursday, finally, time for their planned trip to Alcatraz. She rolled her eyes in the darkness. Could there be any place less romantic?

Still, she couldn't wait. She'd have him to herself all day.

Her phone rang. With Xavier on her mind, she flung out a hopeful hand. She knocked into something and even as her fingers wrapped around her phone, she heard her mother's diary hit the floor.

She told herself it was disappointment not dread she felt when she saw Grandmother instead of Xavier's name on the small screen.

"Hello Grandmother." Amanda sat up on the side of the bed and turned the light on. Her clock read 9:50. It was unusual for her grandmother to call so late. "Is everything okay?"

They'd spoken only briefly earlier this week when she called to thank Grandmother for sending the journals.

"Your grandfather and I are fine. I know it's a little late, but it's well known you city girls keep late hours."

Amanda let that slide as she bent to retrieve her mother's diary from the floor. She flinched a little, knowing her grandmother would be upset if she knew Amanda had been reading one of the journals.

Lying, even by omission, did not sit well with her. She'd been the victim of her grandmother's well-meaning lies and half-truths too many times. But though honesty was important to her, she saw no reason to hurt the other woman.

"I'm giving an extended lecture tomorrow," Grandmother came straight to the point. "I'd like you to come film it for me. It starts at nine. You can come by the house and have breakfast with your grandfather first. We'll expect you at seven thirty."

It was a typical request. Typical last-minute timing. And Amanda usually jumped to comply. The need to please was so ingrained she rarely thought twice. Not this time.

"I'm sorry. I have plans tomorrow."

"Oh." The nonplussed response came down the line, but Grandmother quickly regrouped. "Well, I'm sure you can re-schedule. I really need your help."

"I can't this time. Maybe Grandfather can do it? His last attempt wasn't half bad."

"It wasn't good either. I need you to do this for me, Amanda. It's an important lecture, the last in the series. Now be a dear and rearrange your plans."

"I really can't." Wouldn't. "I'm sure someone in commu-nications can help you, especially if you offer credits for the project."

Silence screamed disapproval for several long moments. "If you're working, of course I understand, but I thought this was your rotation for a free day."

Amanda bit her lip. It would be easy to let her grandmother think it was work, but though her day with Xavier was a re-ward for his speaking at the museum, it was too much of a stretch to call it work.

"Actually, it's a date."

Again a punishing pause dictated Grandmother's displea-sure. "I can't believe you would put indulgence before duty to your family."

"Grandmother, you know I enjoy helping you, but the uni-versity has audio visual people that can help you. I like this guy, and I've already rescheduled with him once." To help her with the reception she'd abandoned him last weekend.

"I must say your grandfather will be quite disappointed in you Amanda. Obviously moving to the city has changed your priorities. I urge you to contemplate your choices so you make better decisions in the future."

"Grandmother—" The line went dead in her ear.

Amanda drew in a deep breath and let it go in a discour-aged sigh. For all Amanda never seemed to please her grand-mother, the demand to try was unending.

Angry with herself for letting Grandmother get to her, Amanda brushed away futile tears. Wishing life had been different, she carefully set her mother's diary on the nightstand.

Unsettled and looking for calm in routine she went to the kitchen to refresh her glass of cold water from the refrigerator. Back in the bedroom she set the glass on a coaster and climbed back into bed.

She was reaching to turn out the light when a knock sounded at the door. Well, wasn't she the popular one tonight? Grabbing her lavender robe with white swirls, she pulled it on over her mid-thigh white nightie and tied the sash.

Seeing Xavier on the other side of the peephole, she swiped at her cheeks, wiping the last evidence of tears on her robe.

Genuine happiness put a smile in her greeting as she opened the door. "Hey, I didn't expect to see you tonight."

"I hoped I would catch you still up so I might see your beautiful face."

"You're so sweet." She reached for his hand and tugged. He cleared the threshold, then stopped.

"The benefit is for a good cause, and was quite a success. However, you were not there. I stepped out for a breath of air and found myself in your neighborhood. I decided to stop by for a good-night kiss."

"Oh." She flushed in delight and stepped back, tugging on his hand again. "Then you should come in."

His eyes gleamed but he shook his head and held his ground. "I better not. I must get back."

"Of course." She fought to contain her disappointment. "I'm glad you came."

"Hey." He cupped her cheek in one large hand and ran his thumb under her eye. "You are upset."

"Not anymore." She ducked her head, a heavy fall of strawberry blond hair falling forward to shield her. But she didn't want to hide from Xavier, to waste this time with him. She squared her shoulders and lifted her chin to give him a shyly bold smile. "Not once I get my kiss."

"Then I must oblige." His hand urged her up as he lowered his head and took her mouth with his.

Yes. The caress started out slow, a soft brush of his lips over hers. But it wasn't enough for either of them. He deepened the kiss as she lifted onto her toes and hooked her arms around his neck.

Opening for him, she welcomed his tongue with a slide of her own. He tasted of coffee and man, an intoxicating cocktail of comfort and arousal. Just what she needed to offset the emotional end of her day.

She sighed when he lifted his head and melted against his chest. "I'm glad you came."

His mouth feathered over her cheek. "Tell me what upset you."

"Just my grandmother being Grandmother. She called and wanted me to tape a lecture she's giving tomorrow."

"Ah, and she gave you a difficult time when you explained you had plans."

"Yes."

"It is okay if you need to help her." He ran a soothing hand down her back.

"No." She drew back, shook her head. "I'm not going to let her manipulate me anymore. She can't call me at the last minute and expect me to drop everything."

"She is family." He said it simply, making it clear he understood the intricacies of family life.

"Yes, so she should respect my answer when I say I can't this time."

"Give her a chance. She has not heard no from you often. Perhaps she will get better with practice."

That made sense. His perspective helped more than routine, more than a cold drink of water.

"I can hope." She feathered fingers through his dark hair. "Thanks. I'm really looking forward to tomorrow."

"Me too."

She lifted onto her toes, kissed him softly. "I really am glad you came by."

"I'm glad I could be here when you needed a friend."

"Yes," she agreed, then she pulled his head down to hers. "But it's the good night kiss I really loved." And she pasted her lips to his.

He grinned against her mouth, bit lightly at her lower lip. "It is my pleasure." And he took the kiss to a new level.

She forgot to breathe as she sank into the passion he ignited. Hands that had soothed only moments ago now glided over her skin, sending shivers of longing through her. She pressed against him, felt his need rise to meet her.

Wrapping her arms around his waist, her fingers dug into the fine linen of his shirt. She tugged at the material as she tilted her mouth under his, nipping at his lip, soothing with a slide of her tongue.

She opened her eyes, drew in a breath, and saw the door still stood open behind them.

"You should come inside," she urged him while moving backward. Her fingers went to his shirt buttons. He took one step forward.

CHAPTER SIX

YES! FINALLY. ELATION sent Amanda's pulse skittering.

And Xavier's phone rang.

They both froze. And then Xavier reached into his coat pocket and pulled out his cell. He read the display and regret darkened his eyes when he looked back at her.

"I must return to the event." He confirmed what she had already guessed.

She let her head drop to his chest, felt the rapid beat of his heart against her forehead. The evidence of his excitement, knowing he'd been as caught up as she had, helped to offset the frustration of being interrupted.

He lifted her chin on the edge of his hand. "I am sorry."

"Don't be." She smiled ruefully. "You told me you couldn't stay."

He kissed her hard before stepping over to the door. "Remember where we were."

"Oh, I will," she promised, following him, watching until he reached the stairs. He waved. She waved. He paused. She waited. He pointed to her apartment and she realized he wanted her to go inside and lock up. She complied, closing the door and leaning back against it. "And next time I'm disabling your phone first."

* * *

As days so often did in San Francisco, Thursday started out as overcast and gloomy, but the morning news said the sun was expected out later.

Amanda had agreed to join Xavier at his hotel for breakfast so she hopped on the Bart. He was waiting for her in the lobby of the Fairmont when she arrived. It was a beautiful old hotel, elegant with a coolly chic décor blending comfort and tradition

He looked right at home in crisp jeans, a short-sleeved red polo shirt, a black leather jacket and high-end sport shoes. She'd advised him to wear comfortable clothes with layers and shoes with a good grip for their trip to the island.

She'd chosen to pair her black jeans with a cream mock cowl sweater over a lavender turtleneck.

"Good morning." Xavier greeted her with a kiss. "You look beautiful this morning."

"You look pretty good yourself."

He ushered her toward the restaurant. "Are you sure we have time for a meal?"

"Yes. It's just eight and our tour isn't until eleven. As long as we're at Pier 33 by ten, we're good."

"Excellent, because I am famished."

"Then let's eat." She stepped up to the Maître d' and they were soon seated in comfortable cream tufted chairs at a table overlooking the lobby. Xavier asked for her preferences and then ordered for the both of them.

"How are you this morning?" he asked. "Did you hear from your grandmother?"

"No, but I didn't expect to. Apologies don't come easily to her." She ducked her head, forced herself to face the truth. "Who am I kidding?" She swallowed hard to dislodge the lump forming in her throat. "She's the one expecting an apology."

His hand covered hers on the table.

"Are you sorry for standing up for yourself?" he asked quietly.

It took two seconds for her to answer. "No." Her self-respect demanded no other response. "I love my grandparents, but I must admit I'm enjoying my freedom from them."

The waiter arrived with their food. He set a full breakfast of steak and eggs before Xavier and a yogurt parfait and bowl of fruit in front of her.

"Freedom." Xavier returned to their conversation. "An interesting choice of words. Tell me about your childhood."

She picked up her spoon, poked at her parfait. "My friends say it was the strictest childhood in the history of California. And that's saying a lot because Michelle—you met her that first night at the museum—her dad was a sheriff and very protective."

"Hmm. I would not take her for a policeman's daughter."

"Right." His assessment confirmed her faith in his ability to read people. "She was a bit of a rebel. Anyway, my grandparents are both professors at Hunt College, a small, prestigious university, steeped in tradition. We practically lived on campus."

"A contained environment." He reached for the marmalade for his toast, and she took a bite of her yogurt, enjoying the tang and crunchiness of the creamy concoction.

"Yes. But strict was what I knew and I wasn't a rebel, so, I didn't buck the system much. The tough part was they made it clear my behavior reflected on their reputations. It was more effective than a leash. Gossip in a small college community is second to none. I felt I couldn't do anything for fear of it getting back to them."

"And to the Dean, and college council."

"Exactly. So I had limited independence, and when I did get to go out, I felt as if I were living in a fishbowl. And unfortunately my grandparents weren't very sympathetic."

"In other words you paid for your mother's sins."

"They miss her so much. And it's not that I want to replace her—but it's been clear to me for a long time that they'll never feel for me what they did for her."

"Amanda, you cannot blame yourself for their short-sightedness. You are a beautiful, intelligent, loving woman. I have always been taught that love is limitless. Mine is a large family, and each new member just expands the love we have for one another."

"That sounds wonderful," she said wistfully.

He bowed his head in acknowledgement. "Yes, but my point is your grandparents suffered a loss they cannot get past. It appears to me they were not particularly demonstrative people to begin with and losing their daughter stole their ability to expand their affections beyond that loss."

Amanda pushed her half-finished meal aside as tears threatened. He was so understanding, she found herself getting deeper into her psyche than she ever had before.

"I'm coming to realize that I love my grandparents, but I don't really like them." It hurt to say the words aloud. And she immediately looked around to make sure neither of her grandparents or any friends or foes were nearby to hear her.

Xavier squeezed her hand drawing her attention back to him. She turned her hand in his, lacing their fingers together. She felt safe talking to him in ways she didn't even feel she could talk to Michelle and Elle.

"Those are valid feelings," he assured her. "But are you okay with it?"

"Yes and no," she admitted. "I have to be because I can't change my feelings. But they are my only family and unfortunately I only see us growing further apart, not closer. Especially if they can't respect my choices."

He frowned and she saw the turmoil in his eyes before he turned his head to look over the lobby and the nameless people coming and going. It touched her that he took her feelings so much to heart.

"Have you found no mention of your father in your mother's journals?"

"Ha." She gave a surprised laugh, the moment shocking her out of her funk. "I forgot I told you about the diaries. And yes, he's definitely in there, but with no name. She calls him her prince."

He choked on a sip of water.

"Oh." She handed him his napkin. "Are you okay?"

"Yes." He coughed, sipped again, and pinned her with a disbelieving gaze. "Her prince?"

"I know, corny, huh. Obviously the romance and medieval ambiance of Europe got to her."

He wiped his mouth. "Obviously."

She bit her lip, and decided she'd bored him long enough with her problems.

"Goodness, it's nearly nine-thirty. We should get going."

Wanting to give him the full San Francisco experience, Amanda chose to hop on the cable car just outside his hotel and then walk the short distance to catch the street car for a ride to Fisherman's Wharf and Pier 33, where they'd board the ferry.

On the ferry Xavier pulled her to a spot on the rail. "I want to see the approach of the island and the view of San Francisco from the boat."

"Okay. But it's going to be cold," she warned him.

"I can see the island just there." He pointed out in the bay. "It cannot be a long trip."

"About fifteen minutes."

"Then do not worry. I will keep you warm." He pulled her in front of him, tucked her inside his jacket and wrapped his arms around her. "Comfortable?"

Oh yeah. The man gave off heat like a bonfire. And his nearness caused her internal temperature to spike, too. At this rate she'd be peeling off layers before she reached hard ground. Or maybe not. A little sweat never hurt a girl when the reward was staying in the safe haven of a handsome man's arms. Xavier's arms.

"Yes," she assured him, kissing his cheek. My, he smelled good—a combination of a woodsy cologne and clean male. It made her knees weak every time she got close enough to touch.

She loved that he was a gentleman, that he cared about her reputation and rushing into a short-term affair. But she'd weighed the options and made her decision. She didn't want to look back and have regrets, she wanted to look back and smile at the unbelievable memories she'd made. Because she believed getting her some Xavier was going to blow her mind.

Learning from her mother's mistake, Amanda took precautions earlier in the week by buying condoms and calling her doctor for a renewal of her birth control pills.

The engines roared as the ferry began to move away from the pier.

She felt his mouth against her hair and snuggled into the cozy warmth of his embrace. Too bad the trip wasn't longer.

The weather wasn't much better on the island, but they got out of the wind to view the orientation video. And then they were too caught up in the history to care.

Xavier really got into the tour. After listening to the audio tour, he found the rangers and drew additional information from them. He found the island's military history as fascinating as its prison history, including its role in the Civil War.

Luckily she found it all interesting and was able to add a few tidbits she'd learned from previous trips to The Rock.

Halfway through the day she got a text from Elle saying she was in town and may be able to be free for dinner. She'd let them know by six. Amanda sent an acknowledgement and saw Michelle also responded.

Amanda hadn't included dinner in their plans, but she was hoping Xavier would want to continue the day together. She loved the thought of dinner with her best friends, their men and Xavier. She had the feeling he'd get along great with Nate and Max.

The day flew by as they tromped all over the island, hand in hand, exploring the lighthouse and the exercise yard, and then walking back to the ferry past the family housing and the guard tower.

She took joy in seeing him revel in her gift. She took more joy in the closeness that grew even stronger between them. She liked that he reached for her hand as often as she reached for his.

Breakfast was a faint memory by the time the ferry returned them to Fisherman's Wharf a little after three. Chilled after the ride on the water, with sore feet and a growling stomach— the sun had not made its forecasted appearance, in fact dark clouds had descended on the city—Amanda wanted out of the elements, to sit down, and food, in that order.

Luckily Fisherman's Wharf offered plenty of options. She chose a cafe that looked out over the water and offered a lovely fish stew.

Xavier refused to let her pay for breakfast, or even go Dutch. So she told him that lunch was a part of the day out.

"Do not even think of telling me no." She shook her finger at him when he got that I-am-male-therefore-I-must-pay look on his face. "One thing my grandparents weren't is stingy.

They gave me a good allowance, that I had nowhere to spend, and a healthy college fund that I didn't have to pay out because my fees were waived at Hunt. I can afford to buy you lunch."

"I would never be so rude as to question your finances. It is a matter of how I was raised. My mother has standards in these matters that she expects her son to adhere to, and paying for the date is one of her unbreakable rules."

A perky blond hostess greeted them and saw them to a table for two. She took their drink order and left them with menus.

"The more I hear about your mother, the more I like her. She sounds like a strong woman."

"She is the heart of our family. My sister and I adore her."

"And your father?" Coffee was delivered to the table and Amanda thanked the waitress and gratefully wrapped her hands around the mug. She ordered the stew with sourdough bread and Xavier chose crab cakes served over rice with a sherry-cream sauce.

"They were childhood sweethearts." He answered once they were alone again. "Both are strong on their own, but they are stronger together. Mom says it is because they grew up together. I cannot imagine them apart."

"That sounds nice. Solid."

"It was a great childhood," he agreed. "My father would do anything for my mother. He gave up a prestigious assignment with the Prince when mom had a hysterectomy eight years ago. This delayed his promotion to Lieutenant Colonel a few years. I asked him if he ever regretted his decision, but he said no. She was more important to him than his career."

"That's a powerful love."

"Yes. It could be difficult for a kid when they united against you. It was much easier when we could play one against the other. Unfortunately it did not happen often."

"Ouch." She winced for him, though it was clear he loved his family. A total soldier, he rarely gave anything away with his expression, but it was all there in the warmth of his eyes and in the way he spoke of them.

He nodded. And then leaned back to make room for the food. "This smells good."

"What about you," she finally gave into curiosity, "have you ever been married? Ever come close?"

"No." He spread his hands in front of him and shook his head, the expression in his eyes cloaked once again. "There was a girl from my neighborhood I dated intermittently through school and while I did my officer training."

"That probably made your mother happy."

"Very." He shrugged and for the first time the gesture had a Gaelic feel to it. "Which is probably why I persevered for so long. I wanted to love her, to have what my parents have. In the end that is what kept me from marriage. I did not feel for her what my father felt for my mother."

"How did you gauge that? I imagine love to be very personal between two people. Your relationship will be very different from your parents'."

"This is true. However, what you are willing to sacrifice would perhaps not be so different."

"Ah." Amanda tore off a piece of bread, dipped it in the stew broth. She got what he meant and asked softly, "You wouldn't give up a promotion for her?"

"It was never a question for me that duty to my career and my Prince came first."

"That would be telling."

"I knew when I could not give her my grandmother's ring." He poked at his rice, and then pushed his plate away. "I thought about it, I knew it was expected. By heeding my reservations I hurt two women I care deeply for. But I could not put my family's ring on Elayna's finger. That is when I knew we were not right for each other."

"Two women. One being your mother. She wasn't very happy with you." When the waitress discretely delivered the bill, Amanda was ready with her card.

"No." The wry look he gave her made that an understatement. "But she understood. She told me when it came to love I should not compromise."

"And you haven't?"

"No."

"That took incredible honesty." Impressed with his brave move, she reached out to him placing her hand on his forearm, feeling his heat and strength under her fingertips.

"Yes. However, her understanding only goes so far. She reminds me often that she wants *petits-enfants*."

"Grandchildren."

"Yes. My sister has given her four beautiful grandchildren, two boys and two girls. Yet she will not be happy until she is bouncing my child on her knee."

She smiled. How funny to think of this intense security man, this soldier with the dangerous edge, being hounded by his mother for grandchildren. It made him seem more human, more approachable. She chewed on her inner lip. She found him nearly irresistible when she was a little in awe of his position and sense of duty.

But today, after hearing more about his family, the love story between his mother and father, about how he believed in the power of love in a thriving relationship, she fell a little more for the man himself instead of the façade he showed the world.

How she admired his honesty. It must have been difficult to walk away from a connection everyone but you thought perfect.

She was in so much trouble.

This thing between them was only supposed to be a fun fling with a foreign hottie. But the more she got to know him, the more she liked him.

She wanted to hear more about his mother—she truly longed to meet this wise woman—and the nieces and nephews that brought a sparkle to his brown eyes. All things that added to his appeal beyond the physical attraction sizzling between them.

"Come." He held his hand out. "I will see you home before I return to my hotel."

She accepted his hand. The problem was she couldn't bring herself to care about trouble.

CHAPTER SEVEN

THE SUN HAD given up any pretense of a fight and rain poured from the sky in sheets. Xavier waited in the vestibule of the restaurant for five minutes for it to let up a bit, but the deluge continued.

Finally Amanda looked at him with resignation. He lifted one dark brow in question and she nodded.

He grabbed her hand and together they dashed the half block to the taxi queue. Soaked within seconds, they were both drenched by the time they reached the line of cars. He held the door and she dove inside.

Happy to be out of the wet she laughed and swiped at her hands and face.

He took a moment to shake off the wetness, too, and marveled at her resilience. A lot of women would be shrill in the face of such a soaking.

The driver had the heat going full blast and still she shivered. Xavier wrapped his arms around her but he was as wet as her so there was no body heat to share. After a while the cabbie came to a stop. Xavier glanced out to get his bearings before venturing into the rain, but he did not recognize the street.

"The street is blocked," the cabbie announced.

Amanda turned to look out the back window. "It looks like

a bus had an accident. A police car and a tow truck have the entrance to the street blocked."

"Why do we wait here?" Xavier asked. "Can we not drive around the block and come up the other side?"

She shook her head. "It's a one way street. I'll just get out here and run for it. I had a really great time. I'm sorry the rain ruined the end of the day."

"I will see you safely inside," he stated.

"But it's pouring!" The pounding on the roof punctuated the fact. If anything the downpour had gotten worse.

"All the more reason to take care." He was not deterred.

Her eyes grew bright at his insistence, leaving him to wonder if no one had ever shown such concern for her welfare. Her grandparents did not deserve such a gift. Again he marveled, this time at how she had turned out to be such a kind, intelligent, well-adjusted woman after suffering the indifference of her guardians for so long.

"I appreciate the gesture—" she touched his cheek with trembling, icy fingers "—but there's no need for you to go back out in this rain. It's only half a block. And I'm not sugar. I won't melt."

He took her hand and warmed her fingers with his breath before leaning close to whisper in her ear, "You are the sweetest thing I have ever known."

Before she could object further, he handed a couple of bills to the driver, opened his door and pulled her outside and under an awning. "I am not leaving you to slip about in this muck." Once he was sure of their footing he asked after their destination. "Your building is the third from the end?"

She nodded and pointed across the street. Keeping her door in sight, he tucked her close to his side and prompted, "Run."

She ran, ducking her head and staying close, allowing him to lead the way. He managed to get them safely inside and up the two stories to her apartment.

Once inside they stood in the small entry staring at each other and dripping. She looked like a drenched kitten, all big eyes and water flattened hair. The corner of her mouth twitched, turning up. And then they were both laughing. She wrapped her arms around his waist and held on, giggling madly.

He held her, shaking with a mirth he hadn't experienced in years. He realized he'd been so focused on his career these last few years, he'd become a bit staid. She engaged his emotions, brought him to life.

✗And as soon as the DNA test confirmed her parentage, she'd be forever out of his reach.

The sobering thought cut short his merriment. He bumped his forehead against hers. "You need to get out of those wet clothes."

"Yes!" She backed up, white fingers going to the buttons of her coat. But she was shaking too hard for her fingers to work.

He gently pushed her hands aside and unbuttoned her coat himself. "Where is the shower?"

She pointed down the hall and he turned her and steered her in the direction she'd indicated. Inside the pink and white tiled room, he reached into the tub and turned on the hot water. Next he grasped the bottom of her sweater and pulled the sodden garment over her head. Finally he released the button, unzipped her jeans and helped her step free.

The fact she made no protest told him how far gone she was. Left in a soft pink camisole and tiny white panties, she shook uncontrollably. Under the camisole and a near transparent bra her nipples jutted against the material, her lush breasts jiggling with the force of her shivers.

He wanted nothing more than to shuck his clothes and help warm her by joining her under the steaming flow of water.

"Your l-lips are b-blue," she chattered.

He had to unclench his teeth to answer. "I am fine. My own

shower awaits at my hotel." He tested the temperature of the water. "Step in. As you warm up, you can turn up the hot water."

She shook her head and opened a cupboard. Pulling out a handful of towels, she dropped one on the floor, and thrust the rest into his arms.

"Strip. D-dry off. You can have the sh-shower after me." Without waiting for a response, she stepped into the shower, bra, panties and all, and drew the curtain closed.

A moment later the undergarments were dropped onto the towel she'd placed on the floor. Leaving her naked behind the curtain. He swallowed hard, his temperature spiking with the image painted on his mind.

He should reject her decree and head back to the hotel, but a glance in the fogging mirror confirmed he was blue around the fins. No, gills? Yes, gills. It was a saying his maternal grandfather, a sea merchant, would appreciate.

Regardless, staying was a really bad idea. The two of them alone, out of their clothes, the chemistry between them stronger than ever—it was a recipe for passion.

Yeah, he'd blathered on about being a man versus a soldier, juggling duty against desire, and he'd stolen a few kisses. But their relations had not gone beyond what was safe. If he stayed that would change.

And still he reached for the hem of his shirt and drew it over his head.

Giving in, because the bottom line was that he wanted to stay. Because every second with her could be his last. He would not lose this opportunity to know her before the soldier he was took over from the man.

The heat against his bare skin felt good, but Amanda in his arms would feel even better. He looked longingly at the shower.

Water sluiced over Amanda. She strained to hear if Xavier had stayed, if even now he was naked on the other side of the curtain. She hoped so. She'd been too cold to be thinking of her seduction plans when she told him to strip.

But now—after scrubbing every inch of her body, chaffing her skin until feeling returned, gritting her teeth through the adjustment of her temperature to that of the water—now she finally felt warm again, the thought of him nude and waiting made her steamy in a whole new way.

She reached for the shower curtain but stopped, slicking her fingers through her hair instead. All too soon he would be gone, and already she cared too much.

Making love would elevate their relationship to a whole new level. Was she ready for the change?

This had to be her decision, one she made thinking responsibly and not as a knee-jerk reaction against her grandmother, or for a sense of camaraderie with her mother.

Searching her heart, she recognized a fear of being hurt. And a certainty that she wanted him beyond all doubt. It came down to what she would regret more—something she did, or something she didn't do?

With the adrenalin coursing through her blood, and her hormones running hot, there was no real choice to be made.

Passion making her bold, she swept back the curtain. And looked straight into Xavier's molten eyes. Eyes filled with a longing hot enough to make her toes curl.

Her only cover the steam drifting through the room, she flushed under his fiery regard. He'd followed her orders, standing proudly before her in nothing but a towel.

Moisture glistened on the wide, tanned breadth of his shoulders and the defined muscles of his chest. Her gaze followed a thin line of dark hair past his six-pack, to the pink towel clinging to lean hips, and down to his long, bare feet.

He should look silly wrapped in the pretty pastel, but it did nothing to diminish his masculinity. In fact, the tented material declared his arousal without apology.

Her body reacted to his, chasing away any lingering doubts. She held her hand out, beckoning to him.

"Let me warm you up," she urged him.

His gaze holding hers, he loosened the towel, let it drop.

She bit her lip. He was so beautiful. So male. She'd never been so hot for anyone in her life.

She held out her hand, thrilled when he took it and joined her in the tub. She melted into him, sighing as she lifted her mouth to his. His lips parted over hers and he claimed her as his.

Time stopped as her body ignited. His kiss held a note of urgency she echoed with every atom of her being. He tugged the curtain over, closing them in a steamy world of flowing water, slick skin, and heated kisses.

Tongues tangled as water rained over them. She traced his muscles, digging her fingers into his back. He held her secure even as his hands roamed with erotic intent. Her breath caught on a gasp as his fingers drove her onto her toes with sizzling sensation.

How exciting to be craved to the point of desperation. He made her feel beautiful and sexy. She looped her arms around his neck letting him take them to the next level of passion.

He gave her everything she asked for, gave her more than she knew to want. As water poured over them, adding a sensual level to nerves already sensitive to touch, he claimed her with raw passion. And she gloried in his abandonment.

She melted against him in the aftermath of ecstasy. Only her heart worked, thundering in her chest, matching the wild beat of his own heart under where her head lay on his chest.

He moved and the water ceased.

She groaned and made a serious effort to lift her head, to stand. Both attempts failed.

"Sorry," she said without opening her eyes. "Can't move."

"I've got you." He kissed her head.

She sighed. He had her.

He lifted her up and out of the tub, managed to absorb her weight while drying them both. Wrapping her in a towel he carried her to the couch where he propped her in the corner to brush out her hair.

And she discovered she'd been wrong. So wrong.

Yes, making love with him increased the level of their relationship, but she had underestimated the full sense of intimacy the experience gave her. How totally connected to him she felt.

An attachment that only grew with his tender care as he dried her hair and carried her down the hall to her bedroom. He set her gently on her feet, loosened the towel until it fell free, and then tucked her under the covers. She cuddled into the comforter with a sigh.

So much for making a responsible decision. She may not have been swayed by her grandmother or mother, but she hadn't been clear-headed either.

Somewhere along the line he'd pulled his pants on, but his bare shoulders were silhouetted against the pale yellow curtains. He sat down beside her, reached for her hand.

"Hey, where have you gone?"

Caught up in the heat of the moment, she'd allowed passion to dictate her actions. Unaccustomed to such want, her body had overcome common sense.

"Amanda?"

"I'm sorry." She focused on their linked hands. "I really enjoyed today."

"But you're worn out and want me to leave?"

"Yes. No." She plucked at the sheet with her free hand. "I don't know."

He lifted her chin and made her meet his gaze. "Regrets, Amanda?"

"No." And she meant it. Her second thoughts were not about regret. "Concerns. Ahh hum." A big yawn interrupted her and she grinned sheepishly. "Sorry."

He pressed a finger to her lips, shushing her. "No need. The cold, dashing through the rain spikes the adrenaline. Now your body needs to decompress. You need to rest."

"What about you?" she asked as he ran his thumb over the palm of her hand. She wanted him to stay, but she also recognized the need to think clearly, which was tough to do with him around.

"I am trained to withstand the effects of adrenaline." He squeezed her hand. He wore his unreadable soldier's face, making it impossible for her to know what he was thinking, feeling.

"You fear being hurt?"

She nodded, wondering if he held the same concerns. Did he have regrets? The idea that he might hurt immeasurably.

"It's okay. I understand if you're tired and want to leave." She bit her lip, suddenly uncertain, and aware of her fluctuating reasoning. But what if the most exciting experience of her life hadn't been as good for him?

"Thanks for taking such good care of me." She wasn't as good at hiding her emotions, but she made an effort, forcing a brave smile.

One dark brow lifted. "Ah, *ma petite*. It is my pleasure."

Abruptly he bent and gave her a savage kiss. She hummed her approval, thriving under his intensity. Totally primal, he kissed her as if he had to or die. It was passion with an edge, a claiming that marked her clear to her toes, which dug into the sheets and pushed her further into his arms.

No longer sleepy, as sensation ignited her blood and sent tingles along her nerves, she arched into his embrace. He had one knee on the bed as he leaned over her. She searched his gaze as she looked into her own heart.

"Do you want me to stop?" he asked.

In answer she looped her arms around those broad, bare shoulders and rolled, bringing him down on top of her in the bed.

"No regrets," she declared and kissed his chest and then his chin. "You're mine for now."

"Yes." A low growl emitted from deep in his chest. "May the Lord help us both."

Xavier woke to a dark room lit by a single lamp with a creamy yellow shade. He tossed back the white comforter with orange and yellow flowers and planted bare feet on a muted orange rug. Along with the white furnishings, it was fresh and clean and welcoming.

Just like Amanda.

He scrubbed both hands over his face. He couldn't believe he'd slept. Being responsible for the Prince made him hyper diligent. He had to be careful who he spent time with and how he spent that time. He didn't sleep with his companions—he hadn't found anyone worth taking that risk for.

Amanda was different. She posed no threat. At least not to the Prince.

She was a huge threat to Xavier.

His phone beeped, signaling he had a text message. He looked for his pants, didn't find them, but located his phone on the nightstand.

DNA results confirm relationship. Bring subject to Pasadonia at earliest opportunity.

Xavier's heart sank. His time was up. There was no question now what his duty was, yet he felt a heaviness in his gut that was completely foreign to him.

He should find her and tell her that she was a royal princess of Pasadonia, that he was her servant, and he would be escorting her to meet the father she'd been trying to find.

Duty was clear-cut, the Prince before all others.

He didn't want to do it. Didn't want to see her face when she learned he'd been lying to her.

Oh he could pretty it up, say he hadn't wanted to get her hopes up if the test was negative, that the omission of information wasn't the same as telling a falsehood, but the truth was she'd see it all as lies.

He understood why, of course. Her grandparents played with the truth, telling her only what they wanted her to know, whether for her own good or their own comfort. That lack of trust and respect made her sensitive to the truth. Anything less than total honesty was a lie.

He had no choice. If he refused to tell her, they'd only send someone else. He would not allow that.

But his protective instincts toward Amanda rivaled what he felt for family. Except there had never been a conflict between the Prince and his family.

Not that he expected any harm to come to Amanda. Certainly not physically, but her emotional welfare mattered, too. Who would watch out for her if not him?

He admired her intellect, her candor and loyalty. She was generous, caring, and brave. What she lacked was any sense of self-preservation. She gave her grandparents way too much control over her. How much would she give up for the father she never knew?

Tomorrow, he decided, was soon enough to find out.

CHAPTER EIGHT

"GOOD, YOU'RE AWAKE." Amanda flipped on the overhead light as she entered the room carrying Xavier's clothes. The one thing she'd insisted on in an apartment was a washer and dryer. "I dried your things."

"Great." He stood and reached for the stack in her hands.

She blushed and busied herself at the dresser, looking for a bracelet to brighten up her scoopnecked black sweater.

"We didn't talk about dinner. My friends Michelle and Amanda are in town and I'm going to meet them at this great Italian place. Would you like to join us?"

His presence loomed behind her and she felt the warmth of him along her back and then the heat of his mouth on the exposed nape of her neck.

"I would prefer to have you to myself." His voice was gruff. "But I will settle for sharing you with your friends."

"I'm so glad." Delighted with his response she twirled in his arms, linked her hands behind his neck. "I really want them to meet you. Well, you already met Michelle, but now you'll get to know her. Wait." She stopped chattering, finally noticing his clenched jaw and the light of battle in his eyes. "You're upset. What's wrong?"

For a moment his expression went ice cold and then he rolled his shoulders as if throwing something off. He leaned down and kissed her softly.

"I am nervous to meet your friends."

"Nice try." She straightened his collar where the corner was turned under. "But nothing makes you nervous. You can talk to me, you know. Am I being a Xavier hog? Do they need you to come into the museum? Or is it something from home? Is everyone in your family okay?"

"So many questions. My family is fine, thank you."

"You've listened to all my gripes," she said sheepishly but she was earnest when she continued. "I've never seen you upset. I want to help you if I can."

She felt his hand fist against the small of her back and then relax.

"It is nothing that cannot wait until tomorrow. Let us enjoy tonight with your friends."

"Are you sure?" she persisted. "I'll be disappointed, but I understand if you have to go."

"I need to be where you are. Of this I am sure."

She lit up at his reassurance, at the old-fashioned phrasing that made her feel special, even when she knew it was probably a second language thing.

"Great. Then we should go." She slipped on a red and black bangle bracelet and led the way to the door. "Don't scare me like that. I thought you were going to tell me you'd been called back to Pasadonia."

Amanda laughed at Nate's dry comment. An ex-soldier turned small-town sheriff, his stoic pragmatism made him the perfect foil for the jaded, artistic Michelle. Just as the reckless hockey player, Max, was the ideal mate for Elle, a by-the-rules, family-oriented optimist.

Joy bloomed within Amanda. Sitting here with her dear friends, with the men they loved, and with the man she loved, was the happiest she'd ever been.

She loved Xavier? She carefully set her wine on the table. "Excuse me. I have to go to the restroom. Elle, Michelle?"

The two immediately stood up. "We'll be right back," Michelle declared.

"Why do they do that?" Nate said behind them.

"My theory is it's a pack thing," Max answered easily. "Ingrained into their DNA from the day of cavemen, when it wasn't safe to venture out alone."

"Creative thinking."

"I can only tell you it is the same in Pasadonia."

Michelle rolled her eyes.

Elle grinned. "They are so clueless." She pushed into the restroom, held the door for the other two. "What's up, Amanda? You were okay and then you suddenly went white."

Amanda paced in front of the three stalls with shiny red doors. "I've done something really stupid."

"Calm down, babe, we'll work this out," Elle assured her.

"As soon as you explain," Michelle agreed. "I was sitting right there and didn't see any stupid behavior."

"That's because it's in here." Amanda tapped her chest over her heart. "I love Xavier."

"Oh, Amanda!" Excited, Elle clasped Amanda's hand. And then she connected the dots that Xavier would be leaving in a few weeks. "Oh, Amanda."

"What am I going to do?" She pleaded for guidance. "I don't want him to go."

"How does he feel?" Michelle asked. "Is there any possibility he'd stay?"

Amanda shook her head. "I can't see where he would. He's a royal guard. His whole career is tied to the Prince. And his family is there. It's clear he cares deeply for them."

"How does he feel about you?"

"I don't know. He likes me." At least he seemed to care

about her. How did you tell these things when it really mattered? He hadn't talked about love. But then neither had she.

Why would they, when he was leaving so soon?

"Amanda." Michelle propped a hand on her hip. "He likes you? Please. The man has been devouring you with his eyes all night."

"Oh yeah," Elle confirmed. "He's definitely enchanted with you."

"Really?" Amanda asked, hungry for reassurance. "No, I know." This when Michelle threw her hands up in disgust. "I know he wants me." Her cheeks heated as she remembered their afternoon play. "But that's lust, right? I want him, too, but what I feel is so much more than that."

"What do you feel?" Elle asked.

"I love being with him, talking, learning things. We have a lot in common. He was upset before we came over tonight. He wouldn't say what it was about, but it matters to me. I've had a really good time, but inside I've been brooding about how he's feeling and if there's anything I can do. He's going home for a week next Tuesday. I keep thinking what if he doesn't come back?"

"Oh, hon." Elle rubbed her arm in sympathy.

"And then I'm sitting there watching you with the men you love, seeing how you look at them, as if they were personally responsible for the end of world hunger. And it hits me that's how I feel about Xavier. I don't want him to leave."

There was no answer for that so silence fell over them as they stared at each other wishing for a resolution. Fighting back tears, Amanda needed to get away from the sympathy in their eyes and stepped into one of the stalls.

Two tears rolled down her cheeks. She'd never felt so impotent in her life. The three of them were usually undefeatable when they attacked a problem together. But love couldn't be forced, and the situation was what it was.

She'd been right to have concerns earlier, but they'd come too late to save her. The time for caution was past. Thinking back, she realized she'd been lost from the very first night.

A few minutes later the three of them were standing in front of the mirror washing their hands. "Thanks for listening to me." She told her friends, "I'm so glad I have you both."

"What about the sex?" Of course that was from Michelle. "Is it hot?"

"Honestly, Michelle," Elle protested on Amanda's behalf. "It's not all about the sex."

"No, but it is a factor. And our Amanda is a little naïve. If the sex is really good, she could be mistaking that for deeper emotions."

Arms crossed in front of her, foot tapping, Elle considered the argument. "Okay, that's a valid point."

Both women turned their gazes on Amanda.

"Oh." Heat scorched her cheeks. "Steaming hot." Literally. "When it finally happened. He was such a gentleman I practically had to seduce him."

"You had to seduce him?" Michelle demanded and turned to Elle. "Does that sound right to you?"

"Max 'the Beast' Beasley, bad boy of hockey, is a gentle, dedicated father," Elle pointed out. "Xavier is an honorable man, here for a short time. Amanda is special. Maybe he didn't want to hurt her."

"Maybe, and six weeks can be a long-term relationship for some people."

"But it doesn't take a genius to know Amanda isn't one of those people, and Xavier strikes me as pretty sharp."

"Hey," Amanda broke in. "Standing right here." Anger snapped in her voice. "If you're questioning Xavier's manhood, don't. He's all man, an incredible lover, and yes, he does respect me. If you heard the stories I've heard about his mother you wouldn't question his restraint."

"Oh my, look at her defend her man." Michelle affection-
ately tugged Amanda's strawberry blond hair. "It must be
love. Here's a wild question, would you move to Pasadonia
for him?"

"Wow." Amanda froze as the concept rolled through her
mind. Her first reaction was no, how could she? Her only
family was here. Her dear, dear friends were here. But then
she considered never seeing him again, and her whole being
rejected the idea.

Stricken, she looked from Michelle to Elle.

"I don't know," she confessed.

Michelle reached for her hand and Elle placed hers over
both of theirs uniting them all.

"My advice?" Michelle squeezed her fingers. "Whether
it's four days or a month, enjoy him while you can."

Amanda bit her lip. It wasn't the answer she'd hoped for,
but it may well be the best advice she was going to get.

"I will. Thanks." She hugged Michelle and then Elle. "Let's
go enjoy our men."

Amanda led the way out and found Xavier leaning against
the wall across from the ladies room.

"Hey," she greeted him as her friends slipped past her and
headed for the table.

"You were a long time," he said, not moving. "You were
pale when you left the table. I worried something might be
wrong."

"Sorry." She stepped close, placed her hand on his chest.
"Just catching up with my friends. Are you okay?"

He pulled her hand to his mouth, pressed a kiss in her
palm. "And the tears?" He gently swept his thumb under her
right eye, rubbing away lingering wetness.

How to answer that without giving up all her secrets? With
a truth, if not *the* truth. She waved toward the table and the
path her friends had taken.

"They are crazy, stupid in love. It got emotional."

The intensity of his gaze never lessened. "You would tell me if you were hurting?"

She blinked back fresh tears. How sweet he was, how concerned for her welfare. Maybe he was a little enchanted.

"Yes." It wasn't a lie. Loving him hurt, but it was also heart-warming, exhilarating, and wonderful. She chose to focus on those elements until she was forced to say goodbye. "Come on." She looped her arm through his. "Let's go home and I'll show you just how good I'm feeling."

Michelle had the right idea. Amanda would enjoy him while she could.

CHAPTER NINE

"THE PRINCE OF Pasadonia is my father?" Shock made Amanda numb as she repeated Xavier's words.

She sat in the muted elegance of Xavier's suite at the Fairmont. A soft blue chair wrapped her in classic comfort. He'd asked her to come by this afternoon after work. She'd been excited to see him and thought they might go to dinner. Instead he sat her down and announced the Prince was her father.

He was different this evening, closed off from her, his expression guarded like when they'd first met. And he hadn't kissed her. Now he'd presented this odd joke. Something smelled off, something that had to do with what upset him last night.

She tried for a lighthearted laugh in the spirit of his joke, but it fell short, sounding like a choked gasp. She was no good at pretending. So she went with the truth.

"Xavier, this isn't funny. I'm serious when I say I want to find my father. Yes, my mother traveled through Pasadonia the summer before I was born, but I'd never claim a relationship with the Prince."

"Of course not. You are too honest, too caring." He spoke quietly, calmly. Not as if he was joking at all. "It is my hope that knowing your mother traveled in Pasadonia will help you to accept the Prince as your father more easily."

"Stop saying that." She shot to her feet. "The Prince of Pasadonia is not my father."

"The proof is indisputable." He gestured to an envelope on the dark wood coffee table. He kept his seat as she paced away. "The Prince is eager to meet you. I have been charged with bringing you to him."

"A dim resemblance to a distant relative is hardly indisputable." Agitated, she twisted her watchband as she paced in front of the window. "If my mother's travels to Pasadonia were so relevant, why didn't you say something at the time I told you she spent time in Pasadonia?"

Something flashed through his eyes, but it came and went so fast she wondered if she didn't imagine the slight flinch.

"There was nothing to reveal at that time."

"At that time? I don't understand any of this. How does the Prince even know about me?" This was unreal.

He rose and came to her, halting her restless movements by taking her hands. His warm touch soothed her and she leaned into him.

"I'm sorry, this just doesn't make sense."

"Amanda." She felt his hand run over her hair before he set her away from him. "I sent him the picture I took of you and Michelle. It was my duty. The resemblance is quite strong. The Prince was intrigued and the DNA test confirmed the relationship."

"DNA test?" She pushed away from him. All warmth drained away. "How? You sent DNA?" Of course he did. Where else would they get it?

"It was necessary for an accurate identification. I know you are unsettled by this news, but there is nothing to fear. I will be with you."

"You stole my DNA?" The words came out raw, but then that's how she felt.

His shoulders went back. "Yes. It was an order."

"Oh." Her mind raced, going over the past two weeks. "Oh." She closed her eyes as it all became clear. She'd been an assignment. He didn't care for her. He was just doing his job, babysitting her until the test results came in.

"Amanda." He tried to close the distance between them.

"No." She backed away, step for step. He wasn't the honorable man she'd thought him. "Why didn't you tell me? Why didn't you just ask?"

"If the tests were negative, there was no need for you to know they were ever done."

"And I could make no claim against the Prince, right?"

"It was a matter of discretion."

"Why are you doing this?" she asked, desperate for an explanation that made sense. "You were upset last night, what happened? Have you been ordered back to Pasadonia and you're pulling this stunt to make it easier to leave? If so, please stop, I'd rather keep the good memories of our time together."

"I have been ordered to return to Pasadonia and bring you for presentation to your father. We shall leave on Tuesday." He spoke with a terrible formality, stiffness in both his tone and his spine.

He was so unlike the warm and solicitous man she'd grown to love it took her a minute to process what he'd said. All her doubts and concerns came back to haunt her.

Except she'd never suspected him of deceit.

"Oh no, I'm not going to Pasadonia with you. I'm never going anywhere with you ever again." In fact, she'd had enough. Where was her purse? She swung toward the chair she'd occupied earlier.

He stepped into her path. "I understand you are upset, but if you do not go with me, his majesty will only send another escort, and another, until you agree to come. Why drag this out? You wanted to find your father, now you have—and he desires to meet you."

"Yes, I wanted to know who my father was." She rubbed at her temple where a throbbing headache had blossomed. Her weariness and disillusionment were clear in her voice but she didn't have the strength to hide her emotions at this point. "But whether I met him or not was to be my decision. I have obligations, a job, family. I can't just drop everything and get on a plane with you." This conversation was going nowhere. "I have to go."

"Of course." But he didn't move out of her way. "Amanda, you are an intelligent woman. You are smart enough to know the truth when you hear it." He walked to the coffee table, picked up the manila envelope, held it out to her.

She lifted furious eyes to him, letting rage override the hurt. "I don't want it."

"I know you are angry with me, but you know I would not lie to you. Read it. Call me on my mobile."

She snatched it from him. Picked up her purse. Headed for the door. "As far as I'm concerned all you've done is lie."

Xavier's hand on her arm stopped her.

She whirled on him. "Don't touch me."

He immediately released her and threw both hands up in the universal sign of surrender.

"I may be a fool," she bit out, holding her purse and the envelope in front her like a shield. "But I'm not stupid. You used me. You—" Her throat closed, cutting off her words. Swallowing, taking a deep breath, she fought for control. "You stole a part of me. You lied. And you used my attraction for you to lull me along until the test results came in. You don't get to touch me ever again."

"I did no—" He cut himself off to stand stoically silent. The only sign of agitation was the heavy rise and fall of his chest as if he exerted great control.

What had he been going to say?

What could he say?

"Was any of it real?" She hated the plea, hated the need to validate a relationship that clearly existed only in her fantasies. Maybe she should have paid more attention to Grandmother. Because obviously she was right, Amanda was too naïve for her own good.

"Don't answer that. Of course it wasn't. No wonder you never made the moves on me. You weren't attracted to me. Oh Lord, yesterday." Anguish gripped her. "You must have felt compelled to make love to me."

She wanted to hide in shame but forced her chin up. "I'm sorry—"

"Do not!" Fire flashed in his eyes but only for an instant before he leashed his emotions once more. "You forced nothing. My feelings toward you are of no matter."

"It matters to me!"

"I should not have touched you. It was inappropriate and I apologize."

Her heart broke a little more with every word he spoke.

"You forbid me from expressing sorrow for forcing you into a difficult position, but it's okay for you to dismiss what passed between us?" Her voice shook with the power of her emotions. "I get to say what is appropriate for me. I am not a citizen of Pasadonia. You are not responsible for me."

"I am a royal guard." His shoulders straightened to sharp edges. "It is my duty to protect and serve the royal family. You are of royal blood. My duty is clear."

"Duty." More than her voice broke on the word. "My grandparents have taught me all about the warmth of duty."

He slowly closed his eyes as if it took an effort to bank the mix of emotions that had risen to the surface. She imagined regret, sadness, anger but dismissed it as wishful thinking. Most likely it had been impatience.

"You and your prince can keep your duty." She stepped around him, turned the door handle. "I don't need it. Or you."

This time he let her go.

* * *

"If you get on that plane, you are cutting all ties with your grandfather and me." Grandmother sat ramrod straight on her cream sofa, her hands clenched in her lap.

For the second time in as many hours Amanda sat stunned by news being directed at her. She'd gone directly from her interview with Xavier to her grandparents' home to give them the news.

She didn't need to read the DNA report to realize he'd been telling her the truth. No, she wasn't dense. But she'd read it anyway. All three pages of it, one with the Prince's DNA graph, one with hers and the third page explaining the validation process.

It wasn't difficult to see the similar spikes on the graph. Besides what would the Prince gain by claiming a relationship with her if there wasn't one?

The Prince of Pasadonia was her father.

She'd rushed to Sausalito to inform her grandparents, thinking they would want to know, hoping for some sympathy and guidance in the face of Xavier's demand to leave on Tuesday for a command introduction to her royal father.

She'd been wrong.

Not only was Grandmother not sympathetic, she was out-right hostile.

"That man stole our daughter from us," Grandmother denounced in frigid tones. "He can't have you. Your grandfather and I have raised you as our own. You owe us your loyalty."

"That man?" Something in the way she said the words made Amanda go very still. "Grandmother, do you know who he is? Have you known who my father is all this time and kept if from me?"

"Don't take that tone with me, young lady." Grandmother looked sternly down her nose at Amanda. "There was no need for you to learn anything of your father. We have provided for your every need."

"It's not a matter of needs. It's a matter of identity. Of knowing who I am, of knowing what family I have and who they are."

"You are our daughter's child. She should be enough for you."

"How can she be enough for me when you horde information about her like she's gold mined from a depleted shaft? As if sharing with me diminishes her in some way?"

"She died," Grandmother said with great vehemence. "Because of you, she died."

"It was my fault." Amanda's shoulders slumped in defeat. She'd always known they blamed her for the loss of her mother and here was the confirmation. "So I didn't deserve to know her?"

Grandmother looked away. "Such a loss is difficult to talk about."

"Why?" Amanda pleaded. "Why was it so hard to tell me about her?"

Silence greeted her query.

"Do you hate me that much?" Amanda whispered.

"Stop being so dramatic." Grandmother leaned forward to minutely adjust the magazine atop the coffee table. "If you must know, she shamed us. Do you have any idea how humiliating it was to have her sashaying about campus pregnant and unwed? Hunt is a small, prestigious university with traditional values. Your grandfather and I suffered censure for months."

It was all too easy to see their reputations had meant more to them than their child's happiness. How sad. And how familiar.

"And my father?"

"Of course we knew who he was. At first Haley refused to tell us, but when the complications developed after your birth, she told me everything."

"But you didn't contact him?"

"Why would we? He didn't deserve you." She crossed her arms over her chest, jutted her chin. "With Haley's passing, sympathy replaced the disapproval around campus and we were able to put her indiscretion behind us. If you acknowledge Jean Claude Carrère now, the circumstances of your birth will be resurrected, and we'll be forced to relive the mortifying scrutiny all over again."

"What about me? What about my opportunity to know my father?" She challenged her grandmother like never before.

For Amanda it had always been about pleasing her grandparents, always seeking their approval. That ended now. The sense of betrayal, compounded by her grandmother's lack of concern, was huge.

"Have you ever thought about what would make me happy? Have you ever put my needs before your own even once?"

"I let you go to that princess camp you carried on about."

"Once. You refused to let me go back even though I begged."

"Because it was a waste. And you were obsessed with all things princess." She sniffed her disdain. "I was supposed to tell a child who mooned over every fairy tale and Disney princess that she was the daughter of a prince who didn't know she existed? Not likely."

"I was eleven. I outgrew the fascination. You could have told when I got older."

"Stop this now." Grandmother clearly disliked being questioned. "This emotional outburst is unbecoming on you. We did our duty. We raised you as our own, provided a good education for you. You should be grateful."

"Grateful?" Amanda asked appalled. "Family shouldn't have to be grateful for supporting each other. I love you and Grandfather. Do you love me?"

She didn't know where the question came from except

when she stopped and thought about it, she couldn't remember the last time she heard either of her grandparents actually voice their affection for her.

"Now you're being silly." Grandmother stood and smoothed her camp shirt over her linen pants. "You're not going, so this discussion is over. We won't speak of this again. It would distress your grandfather."

"I am going."

Grandmother froze, turned slowly to face Amanda. "You're just saying that to be contrary." Her icy tone made Xavier's coolness seem warm and toasty. "I won't succumb to emotional blackmail."

Amanda jumped to her feet.

"Emotional blackmail? I simply asked you to admit you love me. Something you couldn't do." She paused. And still nothing. "Emotional blackmail is telling me by boarding the plane I'm cutting all ties with you and grandfather."

"It's for the best."

"You would cut me out of your lives?"

"You're not going, so it's not an issue."

"Oh, I'm going."

"I said no." Grandmother's tone held steel.

"But you don't make my decisions for me anymore. You kept the information about my father from me. Now he's found me, and I choose to act on the invitation he's issued."

Ingrid lifted her chin. "Then you've made your choice."

"Yes."

Amanda came here to find comfort and reassurance. Instead she received a large dose of truth she'd been unprepared to handle. But she wouldn't accept the blame for the deterioration of her family. Not when she was simply trying to find her way. She grabbed her keys.

"But remember this, you forced it."

* * *

Xavier shifted gears allowing the tension to drain from his shoulders. He recognized the streets and realized Amanda was headed home.

She'd been so upset earlier he'd felt compelled to follow her to ensure her safety. He knew from his report on her that the address she'd gone to belonged to her grandparents.

If she'd hoped for sympathy, clearly she hadn't found what she sought. From the body language he observed through the front window, her visit had been more confrontational than comforting.

She looked paler and even more distressed after talking to her grandmother than she had when she left him.

He wouldn't have thought it possible.

She found a parking spot on the street and he pulled into a loading zone to watch until he saw her safely inside and her lights go on. It took remarkable restraint not to go up and make sure she'd properly locked her door.

And not because of any sense of duty.

He felt disjointed, out of sync, at odds with himself when it came to Amanda. Her safety was the most important thing in the world to him, but not because his Prince had ordered it.

He'd hurt her. It killed him knowing all the misery she'd borne today zeroed back on him. He'd never forgive himself for putting his desires before her welfare.

Drawing his mobile phone out, he quickly dialed a number.

"Yes," Amanda answered, her tone cool as the night air on the other side of his window.

"Are you okay?" he asked. "You had much information to process today," he added to keep her from guessing he'd been following her across the city. "Do you have any questions for me?"

"There were only three pages." No sign of a thaw in her voice. "It wasn't that hard to follow."

"Of course." So it had been a sad excuse for a question. His *maman* always said a poor excuse was better than no excuse at all. "I know you were upset."

"I'm fine."

"Please do not let my mistakes influence you against the Prince. You deserve this opportunity to meet your father."

"Why does it have to be so soon?" she demanded. "It's difficult to make arrangements on such short notice."

"Tell me what you need. I will make any arrangements necessary."

"I don't need you to fix my problems." She bristled. "When do you need an answer?"

"I can hold the flight until eight o'clock Tuesday night." Encouraged by the query he pushed back the flight plan by several hours to give her as much time to elect to travel with him as possible. "Call me…if you need anything."

"I won't—" She stopped and he heard her suck in a deep breath. "Thank you."

"Amanda—"

"Xavier," she broke in. "I can't talk to you right now. I have to separate you from my father in my head or I won't be able to think clearly. I'll call you when I've made my decision."

Silence announced the call had ended.

He sighed and stared up at her window until the light went out. He wanted to help her, to make this situation easier, but he didn't know how.

Finally he reached for the keys and then hesitated. Leaning back he checked the time, did a quick calculation in his head, and hit a new number. A few moments later a familiar voice answered.

"Hello *maman*."

CHAPTER TEN

*We made love today. And it was as special as I'd hoped.
He was gentle and caring, and oh so passionate. He
stole my breath and my heart. I love him. And I can't
believe he could be so tender, so giving, without having feelings for me, too.*

*The girls say it's time for us to move on, but I don't
want to go. I want to spend every moment I can with
my prince.*

*I know we have no future. We're from two differ-
ent worlds. But I can have now. I can make the most of
every day I do have with him. Build memories to sustain
me when the time comes for me to leave him for good.*

AMANDA FLIPPED THE PAGE, but there was nothing more, just
blank page after blank page. No! That couldn't be all there
was. She dug through the box but all the other journals were
from earlier times.

She set the book in the box, closed the flaps, carried the
box to her closet, and thrust it into a back corner.

In the dark, curled on her side, she let the tears fall. She
knew her mother's pain, felt it as her own. Both of them falling for men who could never be theirs, who were not who
they claimed to be.

Why hadn't her mother finished her journal? Amanda had

hoped to learn more about her father, the man who had summoned her to him. How had it ended? Had she left still loving him? Had she ever made an attempt to tell him about the baby they'd made?

Had she ever found out who he really was? And if so, had she been able to forgive him? Or would the betrayal have hurt her so badly she'd given up on any notion of a happily ever after?

"You're remarkably calm for all you've been through." Michelle observed from her pedi massage chair. "If it were me, I'd be faceting a certain royal guard's family jewels into a matching set of earrings."

"You mean cufflinks?" Amanda sat with her eyes closed, body humming due to the vibration of her own massage chair, and thanked the Lord for sending her best friend.

After leaving Grandmother's yesterday, Amanda retreated to the safety and comfort of her own little apartment, where she promptly fell apart. She spent the night crying over lost relationships and brooding about the possibility of new beginnings.

She went over every moment of her time with Xavier wondering how she'd so tragically misread the chemistry between them.

In the end she decided he was the world's best actor, and Hollywood was missing a great talent.

She ended the night pouring her hurt and betrayal, her hopes and newfound independence into an email to Michelle and Elle, before dropping into an exhausted slumber.

Eight hours later a pounding on her door woke her. Michelle swept in, wrapped Amanda in a hug, declared Xavier a bastard, announced Amanda's grandparents had never really appreciated her, and when nine o'clock rolled around she dragged Amanda out to her favorite nail shop for a massage pedicure.

This early they had the place to themselves apart from the three youthful Vietnamese women who welcomed them. One stayed at the reception desk while the others led Amanda and Michelle to the massage chairs and cheerfully went to work.

"No, I mean earrings. And I'd wear them proudly. He doesn't deserve to keep them."

Conscious of the women working on their feet Amanda turned a wide-eyed stare on her friend. "You are scary."

"You bet." She smiled evilly. "Better, I'm engaged to an ex-Army Ranger. You want him to beat up Xavier?"

"Tempting. But I don't think that's a good idea. Nate is impressive, but Xavier is also a professional soldier."

"Nate could take him," Michelle asserted confidently.

"Maybe." Amanda thought of the grace and controlled strength Xavier exhibited during his sword demonstration at the museum. Her nerves tingled at the memory. "But not without suffering damage. It's not worth it."

"As if a beat down was actually an option." Michelle reached out and socked Amanda in the arm. "You're still stuck on the guy."

"I don't want to be. I'd give anything to flip a switch and turn it off." The Lord knows she'd tried every argument she could think of last night. "I'm angry. I'm hurt. I feel used. But, yeah, I'm still stuck on him."

"Dude."

"I know." Amanda sighed. "Nothing about these feelings has been convenient. First they were a problem because he was leaving. Now they're a problem because he wants me to go with him."

But she had her answer regarding his feelings, didn't she.?And no, he definitely wasn't enchanted.

A trill of laughter ran through the room as the staff chattered away in Vietnamese. Glad the women were caught up in their own conversation, Amanda turned to Michelle.

"How can something as positive as love hurt so much?"

"Don't ask me. I'm bemused by this love business more than half the time. If Nate weren't the most dogged man in the world, we wouldn't be together."

"That doesn't surprise me considering your trust issues. The fact you fell for a sheriff, now that was a shock. But you definitely look happy together."

"We are. I can't believe how much I love him, how much it grows day by day. You know the best part? I like who I am when I'm with him. I'm stronger, kinder, more open. I'm just a better person. But you're right, if someone told me I'd marry a lawman after playing second fiddle to my dad's career in law enforcement my whole life, I'd have laughed my head off and advised them to get a brain scan."

"But here you are looking at wedding dresses." Amanda nodded to the bridal magazine poking out of Michelle's tote.

Her friend scowled at the errant magazine and pushed it further down in the bag. "Sorry about that. I didn't mean to rub my happiness in your face."

"You're not," Amanda assured her. "My life may be a shambles, but I'm genuinely happy to see my friends in loving relationships." Did it hurt? Yeah. She'd live through it. "Any advice for me?"

Michelle reached for her hand, squeezed. "Give yourself time. I almost lost Nate because my knee-jerk reaction was to run away. I saw Xavier with you the other night. He's not as detached as he claims. Nobody is that good an actor."

"Yeah, I'm thinking he missed his calling in Hollywood."

"Or he really cares about you."

"It was pretty clear he doesn't." Amanda smiled sadly. "He's a royal guard. He protects the royal family and I have royal blood. A sense of duty is all he feels for me."

"So you don't think he may be hiding his true feelings?"

She couldn't allow herself that fantasy. "Honestly, I don't know what to think."

"And are you going to go with him? You told your grandmother you were."

"That's because she was so dead set against the idea. And I wasn't putting up with that ultimatum." She grimaced. "Look at me, finally rebelling at twenty-five."

"Better late than never," Michelle cheered. "And I really mean that. So you're not going?"

"I don't know. But I'm not going to be manipulated one way or the other. I have to do what's right for me."

"You've always wondered about your father. This is your chance to get the answers to all your questions."

"Yes, but how do I go all that way and spend all that time with Xavier knowing I'm nothing more than an assignment to him?"

Amanda didn't know what to do with her hands. She sat in the lounge of the Prince's—her father's—private jet, waiting for takeoff. Resting her hands in her lap seemed too missish. On the armrests seemed too confrontational. Which was ridiculous—what were armrests for but to rest your arms on?

Michelle brought Amanda to the airport, saw her off at the gate, giving Xavier the evil eye as only a righteous BFF could. Michelle's support meant the world to Amanda. She'd even offered to accompany Amanda to Pasadonia, which nearly brought her to tears. Elle had made the same offer, and Amanda had been tempted, but she couldn't disrupt their lives just because hers was in total chaos. So she'd hugged her friend goodbye and boarded the plane alone.

Now she sat not knowing what to do with her hands.

The problem came from the fact this seat was more like an armchair than the regular airline seats, and the sides were higher. When she propped her arms up she felt rather arrogant, so she took them down and felt too submissive. Better arrogant than submissive, she decided, and went with that.

Where was Xavier?

He'd seen her seated and then promptly disappeared. Leaving her alone with her thoughts, her worries, her growing nerves.

Not about whether to go, she'd made her peace with that decision. Especially after the Prince—her father, as she had to keep reminding herself—called to talk to her. He'd apologized for inconveniencing her by making her come to him but he was unable to get away at this time and he felt an urgency to meet her. He told her of his wife and twin two-year-old sons, saying they were excited to meet their sister.

Sister! It was a shock to hear the word. Of course she'd already learned about the boys from the web search she'd done on Prince Jean Claude Carrère. But it was still unreal. And she hadn't quite related it to having siblings.

Baby brothers, how cool was that?

But she couldn't really claim them, could she?

That's what had her stomach in knots, the uncertainty of her position in Pasadonia. The call with her father had been brief and didn't include any specifics of her visit other than the request to come. She'd asked Xavier, but he'd put her off, which left her to speculate.

Surely they had a plan beyond a broadcast message to the masses that she was the Prince's bastard daughter. The press would have a field day with that. Yeah, she could see the headlines now:

PRINCE WELCOMES LOVE CHILD FROM AMERICA

She closed her eyes. She didn't want to deal with the press. The scrutiny would be worse than the anything she'd ever known on campus. Still, it was better to concentrate on the paparazzi than think of Xavier. And she couldn't think about the call from her father without speculating that Xavier had something to do with the sudden contact.

"Miss Carn?" A voice with a lovely French accent called her name. Early in their relationship Xavier had informed her French and English were the two main languages of Pasadonia.

Amanda opened her eyes to a petite woman in a white and burgundy uniform. Her brown hair was swept up in a sleek twist and her gaze was warm and genuine.

"I am Calli, I will be serving you on the trip. May I offer you something to drink?" the woman asked softly. "Champagne? Or perhaps coffee?"

"If you have it, hot tea would be nice."

"Of course. It would be my pleasure. First, may I show you the amenities on board?"

Amanda followed Calli on a brief tour of the luxury jet. Besides the well-appointed lounge, there was a conference area, a full sized restroom including a shower, and a bedroom with a queen bed. Decorated in soothing cream, gold, and browns, the amenities offered high quality comfort at thirty-five thousand feet.

One good thing about the spaciousness, she wouldn't have to be near Xavier once she had their game plan for touchdown in Pasadonia.

"Your baggage is stored in the closet for your use during the flight." Calli released a latch and opened the dark wood door to show Amanda her luggage. "Please allow me to assist you in accessing the bags when you are ready."

"You've been very helpful." Amanda smiled at the other woman. "I've never flown in such luxury. I feel like a—" Princess. But no, she couldn't say that. "A celebrity."

Calli's eyes sparkled as she nodded. "Let me know if I can do anything to make your trip more enjoyable."

Just knowing where the restrooms were was a help. Amanda needed to talk to Xavier about the protocol and strategy for when they reached Pasadonia. The rest of the time, not so much. Ignoring him worked for her, so not having to ask for directions to the bathroom made her happy.

"May I say I am very pleased to meet you." Calli flashed a friendly smile.

Amanda's enthusiasm in the moment dimmed. Had her identity already been announced to the people of Pasadonia?

"Xavier is a good man."

"Oh. Yes." Amanda relaxed. The woman had mistakenly linked her to Xavier. Her mind applauded the reprieve even as her heart winced missing the closeness she'd shared with him less than a week ago. Except the closeness had been a mirage, made up of wishful thinking and a deliberate charade.

His betrayal stung. How could she trust anything he told her? He was such a private man that she'd cherished every personal revelation he'd given her, especially the stories of his family.

Now she wondered if any of it had been true. Had he made up stories just to keep her hooked? She must have seemed so needy.

"Thank you, Calli." Xavier's deep voice came from the doorway. "Please strap in, we are ready for takeoff."

CHAPTER ELEVEN

AMANDA FROZE. Her reprieve was over.

"Of course." Calli glanced at Amanda. "I will prepare your tea as soon as the Capitan allows."

"Thank you." She watched the woman leave rather than look at Xavier. "Amanda." He held out a hand. "It is time to take our seats."

Ignoring his gesture, she walked past without touching him. In the lounge, she resumed her seat and strapped her seat belt.

He settled in the chair across from her and clicked in.

"Are you a nervous flier?" Xavier asked.

She realized her hands had found their perch, clenched tightly around the ends of the armrests.

"I don't know," she confessed reluctantly. Though tempted to prevaricate rather than show weakness, she chose the truth. Best to keep her own integrity intact. "I've never flown before."

"In that case, we shall endeavor to make it a memorable flight."

She made a conscious effort to relax, but her body was working independently of her mind and refused to give up its hold on her seat.

"The plane is memorable enough," she said with a glance

around the elegantly appointed cabin. "I'll settle for uneventful for the flight."

"A point well made." He stretched his legs out and crossed them at the ankle, the very picture of a man at ease.

The soles of his shoes ended mere inches from her black suede boots. She refused to acknowledge the comfort the nearness brought her. Instead she looked out her window and tensed as the plane began to move. She watched, fascinated, as they slowly made their way to the runway and then came to a stop, waiting their turn.

"Our Capitan is Rod Varela." Xavier chose that moment to begin outlining the details of the trip, including the names of the crew, the flight path, refueling points, time changes and meal options. He talked right through the rush of acceleration and the weightlessness of liftoff.

She looked out again to see San Francisco whizzing by, growing smaller as they rose higher. Enthralled, she sent Xavier an excited glance. He smiled back, then looked out his own window. Biting her lip, she kept her gaze on the tiny pinpoints of lights until San Francisco disappeared into darkness.

Calli appeared with Amanda's tea. The tray included a cup for Xavier and a small a plate of cookies and a selection of crackers, cheese, and fruit. Calli wished them enjoyment and returned to her galley domain.

"Thank you," she said when they were alone. Because of course he'd done it on purpose, overwhelming her with details to distract her from being nervous during takeoff. Between his chatter and the newness of the experience she forgot her anxiety, allowing her to enjoy the moment.

He inclined his head. "I am glad you are enjoying yourself."

"I'll admit it was iffy there at the beginning." She drew circles over the creamy leather of her armrest. She was still angry at him, but his kindness touched her, loosening her reserve. "I keep expecting to wake up at any moment."

He set his tea aside and leaned forward in his chair. His amber eyes searched her features forcing her gaze down.

"I am sure the speed of events has added to the sense of unreality."

"Yes, I barely feel I've had time to think."

"I am sorry. I wish it could have been different, that you could have had more time. However, the Prince has a very full schedule. He has only these two weeks before he attends a diplomatic conference."

Her life seemed insubstantial next to the Prince's. But it was her life, modest as it may be, and in two weeks she'd be coming back to it. This little trip was just a blip in the bigger scheme of things.

He reached out, his hand hovering over hers in an obvious desire to touch, but she stiffened and he pulled back.

"I know what you have sacrificed for this opportunity."

She frowned and looked at him through her lashes. "What do you mean?" He couldn't possibly know what she'd given up to meet her father.

"I know about your grandmother's ultimatum. I know you may lose your job."

She shrank back. Why would he continue to keep tabs on her? Was that what she had to look forward to in the future? Would being the Prince's daughter result in the loss of all privacy? She shook her head. That was one sacrifice she wasn't willing to make.

"Michelle made sure I knew. She promised me much pain if I hurt you."

She swallowed against a lump in her throat. That was so like Michelle.

"It's just a job." She dismissed as if she didn't love her

position at the museum. "And they'll take me back if they haven't replaced me before my return."

Her boss hadn't been thrilled with her request for a two-week vacation. She'd only been with the museum for a year and wouldn't earn a second week for another year. But he would have worked with her.

It was the Director who feared her family emergency might leak into more time and leave them understaffed. She authorized one week's vacation, after which time they would advertise the position. If they didn't hire anyone before Amanda returned, she could have her job back, less a week without pay.

"I can make a call," he offered.

"No thank you." She wanted no favors from him. "I thought you might be spying on me again."

He scowled at the accusation, then sighed and settled back in his chair obviously making himself comfortable for the coming discussion.

"I would not call it spying," he said.

She lifted a skeptical brow.

"I withheld a few things, but I have not lied to you Amanda, and I never will. Yes, I received a slim report of your vital statistics and I had one of my men follow you home the night I met you, but that is the extent of our spying. Except—" He cleared his throat.

"Except?" she prompted.

"I did follow you the day I revealed your father's identity. You were so upset I was worried for you."

She stared at him, torn between hurt, anger, exasperation, and embarrassment. "Your definitions for lying and spying differ from mine. Withholding information I have the right to know is lying. Pretending emotions you don't feel is lying. Following me anywhere for any reason is spying."

His jaw clenched and she knew he wanted to issue a protest, to defend his actions, but he simply nodded.

"Noted."

His capitulation just added to the hurt.

If he felt something for her, why didn't he tell her? Why didn't he fight for her? The answer was obvious. Because he cared more for his career than he did for her.

Calli reappeared to take their dinner order. Amanda had no appetite, but Calli waited so patiently that she finally requested grilled chicken with steamed vegetables. Xavier ordered a steak.

Silence fell, upon Calli's retreat.

Their relationship, sham that it may be, was over. No good could be gained by rehashing faulty memories of the unfortunate affair.

"Was anything you told me true?" she challenged him. "The stories about your family, your career? Any of it?"

"You ask me this when I just told you I have not lied to you?" His brusque tone inferred a strong emotion, but was it anger at her daring to question him or hurt at not being taken at his word?

One of the things she cherished most about their relationship was being able to talk to him. His compassion and wisdom, the warmth he shared from his family experiences helped her reconcile some issues.

It was because of him that she'd fought for her mother's diaries, that she'd been able to learn who her mother was beyond her grandmother's revelations. His steadiness and belief in Amanda gave her the strength to stand up for herself, to truly exert her independence from her grandparents.

And because of him she may have severed her connection to the only family she'd ever known.

No, that wasn't fair. He wasn't to blame for her grandmother's ultimatum, or for the fact her father was a prince in the habit of making royal summons.

But he was here, and he wasn't without fault.

She'd trusted him with her inner most secrets. She'd given herself to him body and soul. Learning she'd been nothing more to him than the next assignment cut her to the core.

He hadn't lied? Please.

His betrayal put her grandmother's antics to shame. At least she never pretended an affection she didn't feel.

"And I just told you how you have," she reminded him, crossing her arms in front of herself, a shield against further pain. "I don't know what to believe."

He pushed to his feet and began to pace the small space. Clearly agitated, he appeared to be struggling with himself.

"*Mon Dieu.* I am a soldier, Amanda. What I am is what you see. I am not such a good actor to be faking things I do not feel. The problem is I was not always the soldier with you. And that was wrong. I should not have allowed our acquaintance to become personal."

"Acquaintance?" She narrowed her eyes at him.

"You twist my words because you are angry. Can you not see it is my duty to protect you? I cannot do so effectively if I am engaged emotionally. It is best for our closer association to end."

"And now I'm an associate." She bowed her head. She'd been right; no good was coming from rehashing the past. What had meant so much to her was disintegrating right before her eyes.

Suddenly he was there lifting her chin with gentle fingers, cupping her face in his hands.

"You are my l—" He stopped, closing his eyes on the searing emotions roiling within him. When he reopened them his amber eyes were more focused but still intense. "You are special. I cannot risk you."

"What does that mean, Xavier?" She pulled away from his touch and immediately missed it. Nothing new, she'd been missing his touch, his nearness, him ever since he revealed the truth four days ago. "Are you saying what was between us was real, because it doesn't feel like it."

"It was very real." He sank into the seat beside her.

Too close, and not close enough. How was it possible to be so angry at him and still long for him at the same time?

Objection, her psyche protested. Asked and answered. She'd put the question to Michelle two days ago. Her friend had shrugged and said, "It can only be love." Amanda hadn't liked the answer then and she didn't like it now.

"But wrong."

"Yes."

"You regret the time we spent together." How many ways did he have to say the words for her to finally get the picture? Why did she persist in tearing herself up by questioning him?

"No." The denial held a bite. "Never."

And there was her answer. Because he was as clear as mud. He said one thing, but his manner inferred another, and now he contradicted himself.

"Isn't that what wrong means?" she whispered.

"No. This is not the right term. Perhaps my English is not so good."

"Your English is excellent. Just talk to me, Xavier." She half turned toward him, her arm braced on the armrest, almost but not quite touching his.

He sighed and moved his arm the scant half inch so his arm touched hers. And when he turned his head, it was her Xavier who looked at her.

"It is not meant to be. I should never have let my personal feelings rule my actions. I noticed you at the opening, and I was attracted to your soft beauty long before you stood beneath the portrait and I saw the resemblance. Of course I knew my duty. I would have kept my distance, but you asked me out. I convinced myself that the chance of your being related to the Prince was unlikely, but perhaps it would be a good thing to keep close just in case. Surely a cup of coffee could not hurt."

She remembered thinking the same thing.

"You were enchanting. My orders to engage you and learn what you knew were a blessing and a curse. It was just what I wanted to do, but for the wrong reason. After that—" his jaw clenched tightly "—the soldier stepped aside and the man took over. Our time together felt so natural. I gave in to feelings I should not have allowed."

"Because duty comes first." It was a statement squeezed through a tight throat. He'd told her, hadn't he, that a woman had never come between him and his career.

"Yes."

Something in the way he said the one word reminded Amanda of a tension she'd noted before, the first time he'd talked about his family's service.

"You didn't want to be a soldier," she guessed.

"What?" His shields immediately went up, closing off all show of emotion. "I am a soldier."

His reaction only made her more certain of her conclusion. "Yes, but it's not what you would have chosen for yourself. You wanted to be an engineer. You're only a soldier because it's the way of your family. For six generations a son has joined the militia. Did you ever tell your parents you didn't want to serve?"

"There was nothing to tell. I have always known I would serve. I have done my duty with pride."

"This explains so much," she muttered, speaking her thoughts aloud. "No wonder duty is so important to you. It's what drives you. Duty to your family put you in a career you didn't want, which only compounded your need to excel as a soldier, increasing your sense of duty to your country and your Prince."

"Amanda, I do not know where this is coming from." There was helplessness in his voice unlike anything she'd ever heard. "Being a soldier is all I have ever known."

She just shook her head.

He didn't even see it, the vicious circle motivated by love, fueled by pride, and propelled by accomplishment. Being a soldier wasn't what he would have chosen, but that only made him more determined to succeed, to be the best.

And their relationship was a casualty of his devotion.

He slid his fingers under hers. "I am sorry."

She should pull back, but this time she couldn't. She believed him. The ache in his voice revealed a depth of emotion his stoic features kept hidden. "I will cherish my memories of our time together."

"So what all this means is it was real, but now it's over."

"Yes."

"Because I have royal blood and you are a royal guard?"

"It is the way of our people," he said simply.

She frowned and then shook her head. Building a relationship with her father wouldn't work if she didn't keep an open mind. But at the same time, she couldn't help feeling resentment against archaic customs designed to keep her from the man she loved.

This was all her fault. She'd known all along they had no future together, so there was no use crying now her expectations had proved true. It hurt more than she ever dreamed, but that didn't change the outcome.

Time to deal and move on.

"Right. It's over." She made it a firm statement as she sank back into her seat, disengaging contact with him. "Thank you for explaining."

"I, too, am glad we had this talk. Under the circumstances it is best we are both clear on the state of our relationship."

"Don't worry," she said stiffly. "I will not be telling anyone about our brief association."

"I will, of course, report my inappropriate actions." He was equally stiff. "But that is not what I was talk—"

"Hold it." Snapping forward in her chair, she sat on the edge and turned to face him. "You are not to tell anyone anything."

CHAPTER TWELVE

"I AM NOT going to start my relationship with my father with this hanging over my head." Bad enough it was hanging over her heart.

"I must report to my superiors. You have done nothing wrong. It will not affect you."

"Your superiors include my father. I don't want him knowing about this. Regardless of what you say, it will be a strain on our meeting. Promise me you won't tell anyone anything."

"Amanda—"

"No. You said it was not the soldier that spent time with me, so the soldier has nothing to report."

"Separating the two is what got me into trouble in the first place."

"Xavier, you owe me." Unable to sit still she hopped to her feet and began to pace. "I get it, we're over. But I don't want my father and half the country knowing about our failed fling. I'd like to be able to look people in the face with some dignity."

"You are overreacting. The reports are confidential."

"Not from my father!" She swung around almost tripping over the boots she'd kicked off. "Not from the generals or colonels or whatever. Your superiors are the people I'll be meeting. I put my life on hold for this trip. Don't make me regret it before we even reach Pasadonia. Promise me you'll say nothing."

He continued to hesitate.

And into the silence Calli arrived with their meal. She rolled in a cart, pushed a button that raised a table between the four console seats, and quickly dressed it with linens and fine china. From a warming tray she pulled domed plates and placed one at each setting.

"Bon appétit," she said with a smile.

"Aren't you going to join us?" Amanda asked, fighting off the mortification she felt when Calli came into the room. She worried what people in Pasadonia would think, but hadn't given a thought to the woman in the next room.

"Merci, I have already dined. Now I must see to the crew's dinner."

"Of course." Amanda sighed in relief. "Thank you, this looks lovely."

"It is my pleasure. Please enjoy." With a shallow bow of her head the woman rolled her cart from the room.

Amanda dropped into her chair, bent double, and buried her face in her hands. "Just kill me now."

A moment later she felt Xavier's hand smooth over her head and two tears leaked past the control she was barely holding onto.

"It is not like you to be so dramatic." His voice was as soft as his delicate touch. "All these rooms are soundproofed to protect the Prince's privacy."

"Thank you God." She uttered the small prayer with total gratitude, slowly straightening in her seat. He was right, it wasn't like her to be dramatic, but she felt so out of her depth. She turned pleading eyes to him. "Xavier?"

"This is important to you."

She gave a frustrated laugh. "Have I not made that clear?"

"It is a difficult thing you ask. A matter of honor."

"It doesn't have to be. What happened between us is nobody's business but ours. I would understand if it was a matter of national security, but it was personal. Not the Prince's daughter and his guard, just a man and a woman. From the moment my identity was confirmed you have been the picture of propriety. Can't that be enough?" She looked down at her hands clasped in her lap. "Meeting a father I've never known is hard enough. Don't make me wonder if everyone I meet is judging me, or worse, pitying me."

He sighed and stood to slide past her and walk around the table to take the seat opposite. He lifted the domed lids from the plates and set them aside. The scent of roast chicken hit her stomach like a brick, heavy and unwanted.

"Perhaps I could delay my report until after you have returned home."

It took a moment for the words to register. When they did, it seemed the perfect solution. She began to slump in relief but stopped. "Perhaps? Does that mean you will or you won't?"

"It means I will, but there is more I must tell you. First you should eat."

Not liking the sound of that, she crossed her arms over her chest. "What more?"

He shook his head and gestured to her plate. "Please eat. You'll feel better."

Nothing she said would dissuade him so she reached for her fork and reluctantly took a bite of the succulent chicken. Excellent. Suddenly starved, she attacked the meal with gusto, mostly managing to ignore the controlling, aggravating, totally gorgeous man across from her.

Surprisingly after the turmoil of their post-takeoff argument, the meal passed in companionable silence. And finally it was over. After wiping her mouth, she put the question to him.

"Okay, I've eaten." And she did feel better but wouldn't admit that to him. "Tell me more."

Xavier went still and then deliberately pushed his plate aside. Running an assessing gaze over her, he saw the meal had done its job in helping to alleviate the tension surrounding her. Good, because she wasn't going to care for this next part.

"You asked if we had a plan to account for your time in Pasadonia. The Prince agrees that it would be best for the two of you to have time to get to know each other outside the scrutiny of the people or the press. This is not easily arranged."

"Of course." She nodded her understanding even as her eyes remained wary. "The Prince is a public figure."

"Exactly so." He appreciated her intelligence, her ability to read the situation. He disliked seeing her in distress, hated he was the one to cause her pain. He very much feared his news would do both.

"It has been known that I would be returning home for the Festival of Arms to see my father honored. You will be accompanying me as my lady friend."

"Lady friend," she repeated, then the light dawned. "You mean girlfriend?" Clearly appalled she shook her head. "No. That's not a good idea."

"It has already been decided. My quarters are in the palace. You will be given a room nearby. Your protection is also an issue. The cover will allow me to stay close without causing undue attention."

"It sounds like you have it all worked out."

Oh yeah. Distress, pain, and a healthy dose of totally pissed.

He could not let her emotions sway him. He was not allowed that luxury.

"The arrangements have been made."

"Without discussing it with me first? Without giving me the courtesy of having a say?" She slowly stood and gathered her personal items, purse, boots, jacket. Her dignity she wrapped around her like a cloak. At the door to the hall leading to the back of the plane she turned. "I'll be taking the bedroom. Next time you communicate with my father tell him so far I'm not impressed."

He winced as the door slammed behind her. Fury clearly had the upper hand.

Bon. He'd rather see rage in her eyes than the hurt that had haunted them, and him, for the past week.

As for her message to her father? He'd be sure to pass that along.

Amanda fumed, pacing the length of the bed and back trying to work off excess energy.

The men of Pasadonia needed to stop treating her like a child. She was an adult and she was past the point of giving up control to anyone else. A lesson probably well learned before she met her father the Prince.

Finally fatigue caught up with her. Deciding not to bother Calli for a change of clothes, Amanda just stretched out across the queen bed in her jeans and sweater and within moments dropped into a deep sleep.

It surprised her how well and how long she slept. And the best part was she managed to avoid Xavier for most of the trip. Where he slept she had no idea, and she didn't care.

If he could so easily put her behind him, then she could put him behind her, too.

By the time she woke they'd already refueled in Baltimore and were half way across the Atlantic. After breakfast, Xavier schooled her in palace protocol and then they were landing in Barcelona where they transferred to a helicopter for the last leg of the trip.

Nearly twenty-three hours after leaving San Francisco, Amanda touched down in Pasadonia. They flew in as day gave way to night. The city sprawled from harbor side to hillside to the beautiful white stone palace overlooking both.

Lights were beginning to twinkle on throughout the city so the landscape appeared to glitter. Amanda's breath caught at the magical impact.

"It's beautiful," she breathed.

"Yes." Xavier's voice came through the earphones she'd been given. "Welcome to Pasadonia."

And then they were flying over the palace turrets and she had impressions of lush grounds threaded with walkways guarded by statues. And the sparkle of water. "Is that a moat?"

"Once a upon a time it was. Now it is just a pond."

Just. As if everyone had a pond in their yard. But then this wasn't just a home; it was the heart of Pasadonia, the abode of the royal family and the governing bodies of the Principality.

Moments later the heliport loomed below them and the craft began the descent sending a sinking feeling to her stomach. Her heart beat a wild tattoo both at the landing and at the prospect of meeting her father.

Xavier assisted her in disembarking and kept hold of her hand. She gave him a look at the odd behavior, then remembered their cover and let her hand go limp in his.

Two people were waiting to assist them, a dignified man with a bald head dressed in full livery and a lovely dark-haired woman in a designer suit. Xavier introduced the man as Armand, head porter, and the woman as Elayna Josef, assistant to the Social Secretary.

"Welcome *mademoiselle*," Armand stated formally. "You have been given a room in the palace. Your luggage will be delivered to your room, if you will follow me."

"Of course." A little loopy from fatigue Amanda fell into step behind the man, wondering why the name Elayna sounded familiar. She slowed her pace falling behind a bit and Xavier matched his stride to hers.

"Social Secretary?" she questioned him. "I thought my presence was to be low key."

"Do not worry. The Social Secretary has no interest in your arrival." He cleared his throat. "Elayna is here more for me. I am involved in several of the festivities this week."

"Oh. Oh! Elayna, your old girlfriend. The one you wouldn't give up your career for." Perfect. Just the person she wanted to meet upon arrival. Someone up in the cosmos had a cruel sense of humor. "Maybe we can form a club."

"Behave yourself." He took her elbow and hurried her along. But she saw the corner of his mouth twitch.

She bit her lips to hide a smile. Sometimes you had to laugh or you'd cry.

As they drew closer to the others, Elayna latched onto Xavier and started talking in a mix of English and French about people and events Amanda knew nothing about and only half understood. Too tired to care, she fixed her gaze on the porter's back and put one foot in front of the other.

Once inside, she followed Armand through wide hallways dressed in quiet elegance. The art was museum quality and warranted a closer look but that was for another time.

"Mademoiselle Carn will be staying in the Champagne Suite." Armand opened the door on a beautiful sitting room in cream and gold, the décor traditional elegance.

"I will leave you here, *chéri*." The brunette interrupted in order to break away. Her brown eyes ate Xavier up, but cooled considerably when she turned to Amanda. "Welcome Ms. Carn. I hope you enjoy your stay."

"You're so kind." Amanda wrapped her arm around Xavier's waist and leaned against him. "I know Xavier was happy to see a friend here to greet us. He's so worried I'll feel like an outsider, he insists on spending every minute he can with me."

"Of course." The woman's frozen smile never wavered. "I will see you in the morning," she said to Xavier before walking away.

Xavier led Amanda into the sitting room where the porter waited. "I thought you were going to behave."

"Hey, I was nice. If my comment showed up her bad behavior, that's on her."

He sighed. "You are right. My apologies."

"Hmm" was all she said, making him frown.

Good. Maybe he'd think twice before defending his old flame again.

"An agenda of the scheduled events for the Festival of Arms is on the desk." Armand resumed his porter duties, pointing out the amenities in the room and ending with the promise, "I'll be by tomorrow to give you a tour of the public areas."

He began to show her to the attached bedroom, but Xavier stopped him.

"Thank you Armand. I will see Ms. Carn settled and take care of her tour tomorrow," he advised the head porter.

"As you wish." Armand acknowledged the change with a sharp nod of his head. "*Mademoiselle* please dial 9 if there is anything you desire."

"Thank you, Armand, you've been very helpful."

With another inclination of his head, he bid them goodnight and let himself out of the suite.

"So what's the plan now?" The words had barely left her mouth when the door to the bedroom opened and a man and woman strolled out.

Just shy of Xavier's six foot two, and broader through the shoulders, the Prince had a regal bearing that radiated power. Dark auburn touched with gray at the temples gave him a distinguished air and revealed where the strawberry in her hair came from. The woman, a slim blonde, barely reached his shoulder and had the warmest green eyes Amanda had ever met.

Xavier immediately moved to her side. Without thinking, she reached for his hand. He gripped it tightly and made totally unnecessary introductions.

"Your Royal Highnesses, may I present Miss Amanda Carn. Amanda, the Royal Highnesses Jean Claude Antoine Carrère and Bernadette Katherine, the Prince and Princess of Pasadonia."

"Oh my." She gulped, her gaze locked on the stranger that was her father. "Hello…" She trailed off, unsure how to address him.

"Papa works for me," he said gruffly and stepped forward to pull her into a hug. "It's what the boys call me."

She nodded. "Behind closed doors, of course."

His answering smile was regal. "I appreciate your discretion."

"Believe me, I have no desire to become the focus of the press." If she thought her grandparents' reputations caused her trouble growing up on campus, times that by a thousand to reach the ruling Prince of a European country.

"Very wise." He held her at arm's length. "Haley's Comet. I'd forgotten her, but seeing you brings her to life again." He glanced at Bernadette over his shoulder. "That was the summer my grandmother had her first heart attack. Everyone was afraid, including me." The Princess stepped forward to lend her support and he patted her hand where she rested it on his arm. Amanda saw now the woman was about ten years younger than the Prince.

"Of course, I rebelled because fear made my parents and the council tighten their controls." That familiar gray gaze ran over her. "Haley kept me sane that summer. She was bright and funny, and so naive. I did not see her in the pictures, could not quite remember the woman who had given me the gift of a daughter. Now I remember. You have her build and her mouth, and she wore her long hair in a braid just like you, though her hair was blond."

"I never knew her," Amanda confessed, tears stinging her eyes.

The Prince nodded. "So Xavier tells me. I will tell you what I remember of her."

"I'd like that." She smiled shyly.

"Oh Jean, she has your eyes." Princess Bernadette stepped forward to sweep Amanda into a welcoming embrace. "I am so pleased to meet you." She kissed Amanda on both cheeks.

She did have his eyes. Amanda had seen it in the photos on the internet, but it was different when she actually stared into them. And saw he was as nervous as she felt.

"Thank you for having me." It was a little lame, but she cut herself some slack considering the circumstances were totally unreal.

They filled the awkward moment with details of the trip and a rundown of events for the morrow. Finally Bernadette graciously brought the meeting to an end.

"Jean, *mon amour,* we should go. Amanda is nearly asleep on her feet. I can give her all this information tomorrow." She turned her warm smile on Amanda. "You will join me and the twins for breakfast, will not you?"

"Of course. I'd be delighted."

The Prince, papa, squeezed her shoulder before following his wife from the room.

"Whew." She sank down onto the cream velvet couch. "I'm glad that's over."

"It is just the beginning," Xavier pointed out.

"Yes, but the first meeting is over. It'll be easier the next time."

"Why?"

"Because the unknown is behind us. Now we can move forward." She ran her hand over the plush fabric.

He crouched down in front of her, carefully tucked a stray strawberry curl behind her ear. "Are you okay?"

"Yes." She pasted on a brave smile. Fatigue and emotion were fast catching up with her. "I'm excited to meet the twins."

"Little hellions. They will love you."

"You think so?" she lifted wistful eyes to him. She really wanted for this visit to be successful. And he'd done everything to help make that possible, aligning himself with her, holding her hand.

"Oui." He covered her hand where it rested on the couch. "Tell me."

She chewed her lip until he swept a thumb over her mouth, tugging her lip free. "Don't tempt me."

Lifting her eyes to his, she confessed, "I just met one of my parents. He remembers my mother. A part of my life that's been blank for so long is beginning to be filled with life and memories. I'm not as alone as I've always thought." Her breath caught. "I'm going to have breakfast with my brothers. It's like a miracle."

"For them as well. I have never seen the Prince at such a loss for words."

"Oh." She'd been encouraged that her father seemed as uncomfortable as she did in the awkward moment of finding family so late in life. "I thought that was good."

"Oui, very good," he agreed and she relaxed.

"I'm so glad you sent that picture."

"Ah. So I am forgiven?"

Hm. Was she that excited, that thankful? That tired?

"No. But nice try." She stood at the same time he did, bringing them kissing-close. Her teeth dug into her lower lip until she caught the glint in his eyes and she carefully side-stepped around him. "I'm safer if I stay mad at you."

A bemused look entered those sinful eyes. "What does that mean?"

It meant if they were going to be playing lovers, she needed as high a wall as she could build between them.

"It means good night." And she walked into the bedroom and closed the door.

CHAPTER THIRTEEN

DEAD TIRED, XAVIER made his way toward the barracks wing. He thought the meeting between Amanda and the Prince and Princess went well. Amanda had been nervous, if the blood stopping grip she'd had on his hand was any indication. But she'd also been poised and friendly. Positively thrilled to finally meet her father.

Xavier was glad to be there for her in her moment of emotional need.

She believed he'd used her feelings for him to keep her engaged while he waited for news that would change her life forever. And neither of those things sat well with her.

He saw her point, but damn it, she should know he'd never intentionally hurt her. Hadn't their time together shown her anything of the man he was?

Maybe not, because he certainly didn't recognize himself.

He didn't allow emotions to rule him. Her insights into his motivations may have struck a chord in him, but he'd never had any trouble distinguishing between duty and self.

Until Amanda.

Problem was even though he'd ended their relationship, the irrational side effects still lingered. He should have been supporting his Prince in that room yet his whole focus had been on Amanda.

He'd laid it on the line for her. A relationship between a

royal and a guard was impossible. She might curse a culture she didn't understand, but she'd accepted it.

It was time he did, too.

He rounded the corner to the corridor leading to the barracks wing and found Jean Claude propped against the wall. He pushed free when he spied Xavier. The scowl on his monarch's face did not bode well.

"You had relations with my daughter." He came straight to the point. The storm in his eyes a warning that anger rode close to the surface.

"I told you we had become close."

"I did not equate that with sex."

"I was trying to be delicate. It will be in my full report."

"The hell it will. Damn it, Xavier, this is my daughter."

"With respect, you may want to lower your voice or everyone will know who we're talking about." Xavier dared the reminder, playing on their friendship. "It is no excuse, but the time we spent together was before her identity was confirmed."

Jean Claude walked down the way and pulled open a door to a supply closet. He flipped on the light and waved Xavier inside. It was a tight fit for the two of them.

"You knew of the possibility. It should have been enough."

"Yes."

Jean Claude's hands fisted at his sides. "You have nothing to say?"

"I have no argument against the truth." Shoulders squared, Xavier faced his Prince. "I can only tell you I was attracted to her before I noticed the resemblance to the portrait. She is a special woman. I tried to keep it platonic. I failed."

"Just so. But you say it was before we had the DNA results. What of now?"

Xavier cleared his throat. "I am an officer of the Royal

Pasadonian Republican Guard. It would be inappropriate for me to have a relationship with your daughter."

Jean Claude's eyes narrowed. "You dumped her!" He paced away and then back, a sure sign he sought to control his temper. "And I put you together as a cover for her being here. Bernadette will have my hide. Tell me why I don't take it out on your pretty face."

"It is a good cover," Xavier assured him. "Yes, Amanda is upset with me, but I am a familiar face. We will deal fine together."

"You had better. I want that report on my desk first thing in the morning."

Xavier held back a weary sigh. "About that."

The Prince had turned away, now he snapped around. "You dare challenge me?"

"I must, your Highness." Xavier held his ground. "I gave Amanda my word I would delay my report until after she returned to America."

"It was not your place to make such a promise."

"No," he agreed. "She was very insistent. Plus I realized the details of the report could jeopardize her cover."

"Hmm." Jean Claude considered that. "Why would she demand this of you?"

"She didn't want to meet someone and worry if they would read the report, especially considering our cover story."

Jean Claude nodded. "Very well, it will be for my eyes only."

This didn't get any easier and it went against everything he knew to deny his friend and leader, but Xavier felt the need to honor his promise to Amanda. She had no one else to take her side here.

"You are her father, sir. She was most insistent about you not seeing it."

"*Mon Dieu,* you try my patience." Jean Claude turned and

walked to the door. "It shall be as you say, but you will meet me in the gym tomorrow morning. We will go a couple of rounds in the ring. I still need to beat you to a pulp."

"I have another request."

"You are pushing your luck, friend."

Xavier nodded, knowing full well it was only by the grace of their friendship he'd survived this conversation standing up. Though not a violent man, when it came to defending or protecting his family, Jean Claude would be merciless. And he wouldn't hesitate to handle it personally. He believed in working his body as well as his mind in matters of strategy and defense. He could handle himself in hand-to-hand combat and with a gun or sword. The two of them often worked out or practiced together.

"I want to tell my parents the truth. You know you can trust them to keep your secret."

"Ha, you think your mother is going to start thinking about grandbabies."

"You can laugh, Papa, but Amanda might not find it so funny. The two are bound to meet several times during the festivities. She'll be uncomfortable if she thinks my mother is building up false expectations."

Jean Claude shook his head and reached for the doorknob. "I barely know her. A month ago I would not have conceived of having an adult daughter, yet in this brief time, after meeting Amanda only once, already she has touched my heart." His gaze met Xavier's, the intensity of his feelings clearly revealed. "Hold your report, tell your parents, be her protector while she's here. But if you hurt her, I'll tear your heart out."

Breakfast with the twins was a lively, chaotic affair. At first they were shy, hiding behind their mother and peaking around at Amanda. Tiny tots with solid little bodies, reddish brown hair and green eyes, they chattered at each other in a language she had no hope of following.

She glanced at Bernadette for help.

The woman shrugged. "I do not know either. It is their own language. I understand a word every once in a while, but I am looking forward to the day they outgrow this stage." She crouched to the twins' level. "Devin, Marco, say hello to Amanda. This is your sister."

Devin, Amanda made careful note, wore a red t-shirt, and Marco's was blue.

"Hi."

"Hi."

The greetings echoed together.

"Hello." Amanda crouched, too, and offered her hand to shake.

Intrigued, the bolder of the two stepped forward while the shier boy stayed next to his mother waiting to see what befell his sibling. A soft little hand settled in hers and she solemnly shook it.

"I'm so pleased to meet you," she said and he nodded, wayward curls bobbing. She lifted her gaze to Bernadette. "Do they speak any English?"

"A few words. Dog, ball, Elmo."

"Ball!" Devin sprinted away, his twin on his tail.

She stood along with Bernadette, and a moment later the boys came running back, each with a ball in hand.

"Ball ech to anda play!" Devin demanded and Marco nodded.

Amanda grinned. "That was clear enough."

"Yes," Bernadette laughed, "but breakfast first." The boys obviously recognized the word and tone because they looked at each other, tucked the ball under their arms, and scurried out the door to the table set up on the terrace.

"They are a delight," Amanda told her new stepmother.

"They are a handful," she replied as they settled at the table. "But also a blessing. And now we have a daughter."

Her acceptance humbled Amanda.

"You're very understanding to accept a grown daughter into your small family."

"Eh." She waved her hand in a truly Latin gesture, before dishing eggs and toast to the boys. "That happened long ago. I must tell you Jean Claude was shaken when he received the picture Xavier sent. For both your sakes I am glad he remembers your mother."

"Me too. The loss hurt my grandparents a lot, so they rarely speak of her. I'm excited to talk to someone who knew her."

A lidded cup of juice shot across the table. Amanda snagged it before it rolled off the edge and handed it back to Marco with a grin.

"Of course you are." Bernadette smiled her thanks. "But what of her friends? Jean Claude said she traveled with several friends that summer."

"I never met them."

"This is too sad. A girl needs her mother." She reached for Amanda's hand. "I know I cannot take the place of your mother, but I hope you will consider me your friend."

"I'd like that a lot." The openness of these people stunned her. "I must confess I expected a much more formal environment."

"*Oui,* much of our lives is formal, with many rules guiding our conduct. You will see much of this over the next couple of weeks."

"Mon amour." A deep voice came from the terrace doorway. "You are scaring the child. In these rooms we are family."

"Papa! Papa!" The boys shrieked their joy at their father's appearance.

"Papa." Amanda gave him a big grin and wiggled in her

seat like the boys were doing. She noted Xavier's presence, including a bruise high on his left cheek, but otherwise ignored him.

Jean Claude grinned back and tugged on her ponytail.

"You made it." Bernadette rose and walked into Jean Claude's embrace. "Can you stay?"

"Only for a few minutes. I wished to be here when Amanda met our little carpet mice."

"Mice?" Bernadette's eyes widened and she looked frantically about. "We have mice? Xavier please call housekeeping. I do not want rodents around the children."

Amanda laughed. "I think he meant rug rats. It's an affection term for children in America. The boys and I are becoming fast friends. We're going to play ball in a bit."

"Yes, I meant this rug rats. Sorry to upset you, *chérie*."

"Rug rats?" Bernadette huffed back to her seat. "I do not like this term. We will not use it to describe our beautiful children."

"No, *chérie*." Jean Claude bent and kissed Bernadette's hair. "My apologies." He crouched between the boys and they jabbered at him as he kissed each in turn. "These two will be your friends forever if you chase the ball with them."

"It's a plan." Amanda could think of nothing she'd rather do.

"But we must leave time to shop," Bernadette interjected. "As he is not a woman, it is my guess that Xavier did not properly inform Amanda of what she would need in the way of a wardrobe for the festivities this week." She turned to Amanda. "Did you know there is to be a ball?"

Amanda felt her eyes widen. "As in fancy dresses and dancing?"

"Oh yes, exactly so. See, I knew this would happen." She clapped her hands, clearly delighted. "We will go shopping, *oui*. It will be my pleasure to outfit my new daughter."

"Oh but—" Amanda's protest was cut off.

"Amanda." Bernadette placed her hand over Amanda's on the table. "You dropped everything when Jean Claude asked you to come so soon. Let me do this for you."

"Really, it's not necessary." She was adamant. After exchanging a helpless glance with Xavier, she explained, "I didn't come to take from you. I just want to get to know you."

"Of course. Just as I wish to get to know you. Let us do this for you," Jean Claude insisted. "I have missed twenty-five years of spoiling you."

Longing weakened her resolve. Nobody had ever cared enough to spoil her, to give beyond what was necessary, just to make her happy.

"But we can't just go shopping. Bernadette is the Princess, wouldn't it be odd for just the two of us to go out together?"

"Unfortunately yes," Bernadette confirmed. "Though I would enjoy it very much. We will ask a few other guests to join us and all will be well."

"Excellent. It is settled." Her father announced and for the first time Amanda heard the Prince speaking, a powerful man used to getting his own way.

"It's too much," Amanda said as she handed Xavier the latest bag from the latest high-end boutique. "She's out of control."

"Bernadette is having fun. It is only a few clothes."

"It's thousands of dollars! For a week's worth of clothes."

"She can afford it."

"That's not the point."

"She has also treated others in the party." He took her arm and led her outside for some air. "What is the real problem?"

She sighed. He knew her too well. "This isn't what I want from them."

"They know this," he assured her.

He said something to one of the royal guards standing

sentinel outside the store and then walked across the way to a coffee house. Inside he spoke to the manager and arranged for a section to be secured for the Princess's party. Once seated, he gave her his full attention. "What has changed since this morning?"

The waitress arrived with their coffees. Amanda gratefully sipped her chocolate hazelnut blend. Avoiding his eyes, she admitted, "Carlo Sainz doesn't like me." The constant censure in the Social Secretary's gaze made it clear he believed she overstepped her place.

"Carlo does not know you." Xavier ran his thumb over her knuckles, his touch every bit the distraction he hoped it would be. "He is a man who likes to be in control. Do not let him upset you."

Sending Xavier a chiding glance, she removed her hand from his touch.

"He does upset me. He made it clear he was unhappy to see me included in the shopping party. I feel as though I'm bringing undue attention to myself."

"He is only unhappy because you have no political connection he can exploit in the media. He knows Bernadette included you because you are my guest and I was given the assignment. Elayna said she would find an angle he would like."

"Elayna?" Somehow Amanda wasn't reassured by the woman's involvement. Carlo's attitude was general displeasure. As Xavier's new love interest, Elayna had specific reason to dislike Amanda. "She really doesn't like me."

He reclaimed her hand, planted a heated kiss in the palm. When she glared her dissatisfaction, he leaned close to kiss the corner of her mouth. "If you want to dispel curiosity, then I suggest you remember we are supposed to be lovers who have found a moment to be together. It would be best not to look as if you wish to gut me like a fish."

He had a point, but that only made her want to punish him.

And what better way than by playing along? He was so close she had only to tilt her head and press her lips against his.

He went still, obviously surprised by her aggression. But he quickly adjusted. From one heartbeat to the next, he went from frozen to steaming hot, angling his mouth over hers and sinking into her.

Maybe this hadn't been her best idea.

Then his tongue tangled with hers and she thought it was her best idea ever.

Heat deepened and bloomed between them. And suddenly the last week disappeared and they were just a man and a woman acting on a mutual attraction. It felt too good to care, and she snuggled into his strength, letting him chase away her worries.

"Uh oh," a female voice twittered. "Maybe we should give them a little privacy."

Her pulse already tripping at triple speed, being caught necking by the Princess's shopping buddies sent heat flooding to cheeks already hot from passion. Instinctively Amanda pulled back, but Xavier followed, drawing the kiss out, putting on a good show for the ladies.

But at the same time it felt so real, too much of a good thing, when Amanda needed to remember anything between them was over. No matter how she might wish it was different.

"We are in a public coffee house, there is no privacy." Bernadette's tone clearly stated there would be no leaving the lovers alone. "Ah, our refreshments. What a lovely assortment of coffees, teas and pastries."

This time Amanda put more effort into ending the embrace. When he sat back, she was happy to see the attention had shifted away from Commandant LeDuc and his guest to the elaborate display the proprietor had provided for the royal shopping party. A six foot long cart held a variety of teas and coffees and a hostess stood nearby with flavor blends and whipped cream at the ready. Waiter after waiter arrived with trays of fruits, pastries, and sandwiches.

Chatter quieted as moans of delight filled the room. Xavier met her gaze and lifted one dark brow. "Maybe we should leave them alone?"

She chuckled aloud, drawing the party's regard once again. Luckily the Princess's guests were a friendly crowd and with indulgent smiles they turned back to their own conversations.

Except for Elayna, who had wiggled her way into the event as Carlo's spy. She glared from the corner where she sat with Bernadette's aunt and young cousin. Xavier's ex hadn't taken her eyes off them since she joined the group. The critical scrutiny was getting old.

"How much longer do you think this trip will last?" she demanded of Xavier.

He shrugged. "This is not my usual detail. You would probably have a better idea than I."

She sighed. "It could be a while, then. I haven't found a ball gown yet. Correction, I have found a ball gown, but nothing Bernadette has given a nod to. She's determined I have something special for the occasion and I'll know it when I see it."

Amanda admitted the idea of wearing a special dress at a ball given at the Prince's palace sent shivers of childish delight all through her. She'd be having the time of her life if it were just her and Bernadette.

Unfortunately it wasn't just the two of them and Amanda felt out of place and on display.

"Hopefully it will be done by three. I have fencing training with my father. He is part of a demonstration planned for later this week."

"Really?" Amanda perked up. "Is that on my agenda? Your talk at the museum was fascinating. I'd love to see a real match."

"I will make sure you get a pass."

"Good." She swirled her coffee mug. "If only finding my gown could be so easy."

A short while later the group split up as Bernadette's aunt and cousin elected to return to the palace. Several of the other guests chose to join them, Elayna included. The sparkle in Bernadette's eyes reflected her satisfaction as she, Amanda, and the ambassador to Spain strolled to the next boutique under the eagle eye of Xavier and a fellow guard.

Bernadette linked arms with Ana, the ambassador, a slender woman with short salt and pepper hair and ageless skin, and the two put their heads together discussing their next stop. Ana spoke with a strong accent but had a delightful sense of humor.

Amanda followed along, conscious of Xavier at her side, of the taste of him still in her mouth. Every moment she was with him yet not, hurt just a little more. She longed for his touch, longed to stroll the pretty streets of Pasadonia just so she could touch him.

Luckily they arrived at their destination, cutting off the inappropriate yearnings. Happy for the distraction, she stepped into a boutique with a bohemian vibe. Not at all what she'd been expecting.

The items on display were gorgeous, colorful or earthy in fabrics that hung and draped beautifully. They made the hanger look good, and on a body they would be nothing short of amazing. But not where she'd look for a ball gown.

And she'd be wrong.

Bernadette and Ana led Amanda into an alcove filled with an array of one-of-a-kind gowns in a rainbow of colors in every lush material she knew of. In awe at the choice spread before her, she stood arm to arm with her cohorts, surveying the selection.

Behind them Xavier stood, arms crossed, eyes on the room. He'd already made a tour of the shop, positioned the second guard at the rear exit and called the driver to advise him of the address of the store.

"Oh, Amanda!" Excitement alive in her voice, Bernadette stepped forward and reached for a gown that shimmered among the dresses. Ana rushed to help her, catching the bottom of the gown and letting it flow over her arms.

With a smile, Bernadette carefully handed Amanda the armful of satin.

"Oh my," she breathed. Her heart skipped just looking at the dress. Her gaze met her stepmother's. She'd been right. Amanda knew as soon as she saw the dress. And yes, it was special.

CHAPTER FOURTEEN

"I'M GOING TO meet your parents?" Anxiety rang in Amanda's question as they wove their way through the mass of tables in the banquet hall headed toward table nine. "You didn't tell me I'd be meeting your parents. You needed to warn me. I might have worn something different. Maybe the sapphire cowl neck dress."

She had to be joking. He couldn't look at her in the figure-hugging emerald green dress for more than a few minutes at a time or he risked embarrassing himself in front of his fellow officers and their families. He tore his gaze away from the sweet shape of her derrière and the way the filmy skirt that started mid-thigh flirted with her spectacular legs.

"You look fabulous," he said grudgingly and leaned forward to whisper, "consider this your warning. Hello *Maman, Père.*"

She sent him a furious glare before turning a stunning smile on his folks. "Mr. and Mrs. DeLuc, it's so nice to meet you."

His father, an older edition of Xavier, stood and bowed over Amanda's hand while Xavier bent over his mother to kiss her cheek.

"Ms. Carn, the pleasure is ours. It is so good to see Xavier has finally found a woman to share his life with. Please call us Maman and Père."

"Oh." Amanda's smile froze and her gaze found his. Too poised to show her dismay to his parents, her eyes promised swift retribution if he didn't handle this quickly.

"Pay no attention to my father." Xavier seated her next to his mother. "He is the devil and you cannot trust a word he says."

His father laughed heartily and resumed his seat. "A man can hope. Your mother worries for your happiness and longs for little Xaviers to bounce on her knee. Such a beautiful woman will make handsome sons."

Amanda choked on the sip of water she'd taken.

Xavier patted her back while sending his father a cease and desist stare.

"My dear." His mother laid her hand over Amanda's and took advantage of the fact they were the only ones at the table to explain. "Philippe teases you. Xavier has told us of you and the importance of your visit. We are delighted to assist in any way we can. Please call me Yvette—and my so amusing mate is Philippe."

Amanda looked to him for clarification. He nodded. "Jean Claude gave his approval."

She visibly relaxed. Turning her hand over, she squeezed his mother's fingers. "Yvette, you don't know what a relief it is to hear that. It's very wearing to keep up a constant pretense."

"I can only imagine. You must put it aside for the next few hours and simply be yourself. Xavier told me of your trip to the prison island. I have heard this place is haunted."

"I've heard that too. I went on the night tour once. I'm not going to say I saw any ghosts, but it was spooky."

The women chatted, quickly becoming fast friends. Xavier took satisfaction in seeing the ease settle into Amanda's features, her posture, her laugh. The meeting with her new family seemed to be going well, but there were expectations and hopes linked to the growing relationship that kept all parties slightly on edge.

With his parents none of that applied. She was having fun. And he found an ease of his own when she turned a genuine smile on him.

The Secretary of Military Affairs stepped onto the stage in front of the insignia of the Royal Pasadonian Republican Guard and began an inspirational speech in appreciation for sacrifice and dedication of the corps.

As the room fell silent except for the speaker, Xavier put his arm along the back of Amanda's chair and rubbed his mother's shoulder in gratitude. He could always count on her.

His father caught Xavier's gaze and winked.

In that moment he felt truly blessed in his family. The question was if he let Amanda go, would he ever again find a love as true as his parents'?

"En garde." The referee brought the fencers to the center of the mat; they saluted each other and then took their stances. The referee stepped back and gave the call. *"Allez!"*

Amanda sat on the edge of her seat watching the fencing match begin. The two powerful combatants lunged and parried, advancing and retreating in a dangerous dance for supremacy.

Xavier had explained the fencing matches were nine minutes long, broken into three sessions with one minute breaks.

This was Philippe's big match and it was immediately apparent these were by far the most skilled of the champions fighting today. Philippe needed to be on his game.

She tore her gaze from the action to check the entrance and then search the competitors ringing the competition floor.

A hand on her arm made her jump. She swung to face Yvette LeDuc. Amanda had been thrilled to see Xavier's mother in the seat next to hers. She genuinely liked the woman plus she truly appreciated being able to be herself and put all pretenses aside.

"Why do you fidget?" she asked. "Who do you watch for?"

Amanda flushed as she confessed she was looking for Xavier. Could she be more of a heartsick loser?

"He said he had a match today." She focused on the flash of steel below her. "I must have missed it. But I thought he'd come out to see his father's bout."

Yvette laughed. "Amanda, Xavier is here. I thought you knew." She nodded to the combatants. "He's there. The current champion taking on his father, the past champion. They are magnificent, are they not?

She turned back to the match and Amanda also focused her attention on the fighters. The men were fully engaged looking for an opening to strike.

"I am sorry." Yvette patted her hand on the armrest they shared. "I forget you do not speak our language so good. Philippe's opponent was to be a surprise until announced at the match. Obviously that son of mine did not tell you he would be facing his father today."

"No." Amanda narrowed her eyes, watching the intricate ballet of strength and strategy playing out in front of her. "He did not."

She'd followed the introductions well enough to know Philippe wore the gold armband, which meant Xavier wore the red. She realized she'd been so busy looking for him she'd missed his entrance. And then the audience reacted so strongly when he was announced she hadn't heard his name.

He moved with such grace and fluidity her eye had been drawn to him before she'd even known it was Xavier. Now she knew she couldn't take her eyes off him.

When the match started, she'd worried that this aggressive opponent might best Philippe. And he might, which left her torn. She didn't want either to lose.

The first break was called with no score, a testament to their skill.

"How can you stand it, knowing one of them will lose? Won't there be hard feelings between them?"

Yvette shook her head. "As long as it is well fought, they will be fine." She sent Amanda an arch glance. "And the loser will already be looking forward to the next battle and his chance at victory."

Amanda laughed. "That I believe."

"You care for him." The statement from Yvette held a wealth of knowledge, of compassion.

"I love him," she admitted as the next round began.

She thought of denying her feelings, but why? She was a terrible liar. His mother was sharp, she'd see through Amanda in a heartbeat.

And when Yvette turned her wise amber eyes on Amanda, she was glad she'd been honest. Already she valued this woman as a friend. She hoped Xavier realized how lucky he was.

"He cares for you, too," Yvette assured her.

"Not enough."

"How much would be enough?"

Good question. What did she expect from Xavier? That he'd give up a career steeped in family history? Or turn his back on the country he put his life on the line for? Wave good-bye to a family he obviously adored?

As she watched, he parried and thrust, forcing Philippe on the defense. The stamina required for the sport astounded her.

"Too much," she finally answered Yvette's question, her throat closing around the words. "There's too much to overcome. I knew that from the beginning."

"If you knew this, why did you start something with him?"

Wow. Enough with the tough questions already.

"Because he was gorgeous, and fascinating, and attentive. He's so far out of my league. I mean look at him." She gestured to the floor where Xavier wielded a sword as if it were an extension of his arm. "But he made me feel special."

"To him you are special."

The second break came with a score of one to nothing, Philippe managing to make one hit.

Tense with the action on the floor and the conversation in the seats, Amanda sat straighter in her seat and turned her head to look at Yvette.

Amanda shook her head. "He had orders."

"Which he jeopardized by spending time with you."

"What? No." That wasn't right. She knew exactly what his orders had been. His words were burned into her brain. "He was supposed to keep tabs on me, find out what I knew about my father."

"You think he pretended interest in you to facilitate his orders." Again it was a statement, not a question. Her eyes were steady on Amanda's when she said, "This is not Xavier's way."

"Yvette." Of course his mother didn't want to think her son had led a woman on. Everything he'd told her about Yvette spoke against such treatment.

"Amanda, my son is a professional soldier. He knows how to keep someone under surveillance and extract information without kissing them."

Xavier *was* a professional. His seriousness and sense of duty were the first and last things you noticed about him.

"He is one of the youngest men to reach the rank of Commandant in the history of the corps. We are very proud of him. He has achieved this through his dedication to his career and to the crown."

She knew all this, or at least wasn't surprised by it. Everything his mother just explained was what was keeping them apart. Yet Yvette's earnest expression indicated she was trying to tell Amanda something.

"I don't understand." She shrugged helplessly. "Every point you've made only seems to highlight our obstacles."

"Exactly." Yvette patted her arm as if she were the most clever of women. "Xavier is a soldier, so the question is why did he not do his duty as he should? I think because he could not. Because Xavier the man saw someone he wanted and he acted on that desire."

A collective gasp from the audience snapped her attention back to the match. The last period had begun and Philippe was on the attack, pushing Xavier to the edge of the mat, the sword action more heard than seen. Xavier held his ground, forcing Philippe back with sheer brute strength and a feint that allowed him to gain an advantage.

"Breathe, child," Yvette advised beside her. "It is not life or death."

"It feels like it is." Amanda took a breath. "Those are sharp weapons they're using. Even with the masks and suits, it's unnerving to watch."

"There is much about being a soldier's wife that is unnerving."

Another shot to the gut. For a sweet woman, Xavier's mother played hardball.

"I imagine that's true." But she hadn't really given it much thought. Because much as she loved him, she couldn't see the future for the obstacles in their way. Often soldiers' wives had to give up everything to follow their man.

Keeping in touch with friends and family wasn't as difficult as in past eras, but there was still sacrifice. All impediments aside, could she be a soldier's wife?

The question deserved more than a second's reflection but her gut answer said yes. She knew how it felt to long for something with all her heart and the loneliness of feeling as if part of her life was missing.

Yes, a soldier's life involved risk, but life was full of uncertainties. In truth, you never knew how long you'd have with someone. She'd rather grab what time she could with her love and live life to the fullest every day, than shrink from the thought of loss and face eternal regret.

The match ended with a ring of steel as the referee called halt. Philippe's one point made him the winner and the crowd cheered as the son bowed to the father in acknowledgement of the victory.

Sweat drenched Xavier's dark hair, evidence of the work-out he'd just had, but the wide smile on his face reassured her he'd enjoyed the match. And then he looked right at her, that brash smile still on his face, and waved. She froze, as heads turned in her direction, being acknowledged by the reigning champion was hardly low profile. Thankfully Yvette waved back, dispelling a lot of the interest.

But the persistent man continued to watch her so she gave a little wave. His grin broadened and then he was swept away as the emcee wrapped up the demonstration by presenting Philippe with a handsome plaque.

Yvette nudged Amanda with her elbow. "My man won."

Amanda nudged her back with a smile. "I thought you didn't care who won."

Her eyes sparkled. "I have a slight preference. I love my son, but one thing I have learned over many years of marriage is to put Philippe before all others. When we are together, everything else falls into place."

"That's really lovely."

Yvette's smile held a rueful edge. "The truth is we are stronger together than apart. I will not lie, sometimes it is an effort. But it is always worth it."

"Anda. Anda ball!" Devin called before launching his ball at Amanda.

"Got it, yeah!" She made a big deal of catching the ball. In jeans and an aqua t-shirt, she enjoyed a few minutes with her brothers before she had to dress for tonight's ball.

"Yeah!" Marcus crowed. "Anda, cach." And he threw his ball.

"Goodness." She opened her arms for the lob coming her way and ended up bobbling the two balls. In the end she threw up her arms and let the two balls tumble to the ground.

The boys giggled and scurried after the rolling balls. She plopped on the grass of the inner courtyard and watched her brothers chase balls and each other around the manicured lawn.

Each day she tried to spend some time with them. They loved being outdoors and this was a somewhat public spot where they could appear to cross paths. Their nanny sat nearby and a guard stood at a discreet distance.

A ball rolled close. She picked it up and tossed it from one hand to the other until Marcus came running. He stopped and held his arms up and she gently tossed it to him. It fell through his arms and he scurried after it.

She leaned back on her arms and waited for the next round of ball. Boot-clad feet appeared in her peripheral vision and she looked up the long, lean length of Xavier. Like the Secret Service back home, the Royal Guard wore black suits and ties, which allowed them to be less obtrusive in guarding the Prince or visiting dignitaries.

His shoulders appeared a mile wide. And though the formal look lent him an austere aura meant to intimidate, she remembered the hard body beneath the dark material and how it felt to be in his arms.

The hot intensity in his eyes made her think he was remembering the same thing.

Putting the dangerous thought aside, she patted the grass beside her. "Have a seat."

This past week had been one frustrating moment after another as they played the part of lovers in public and platonic friends in private. Not that there were many private moments. Something she was sure Xavier deliberately arranged. Being alone with her was something he avoided at all cost.

But if she thought the invitation would chase him away, she was doomed to disappointment. He shrugged off his jacket, tossed it to the ground, and casually dropped down beside her. Like her, he watched the boys running wild.

"They are hard to resist, are they not?"

That quick emotion clogged her throat. "I love them already."

"So, you are glad you came?"

"Yes." No hesitation there. She'd found the family, the warmth of approval she'd always longed for here. She and Bernadette were already fast friends and the affection between her and her father grew daily. It made it hard to think of leaving.

"Thank you for convincing me to come."

"You convinced yourself. You are a strong, smart woman. Brave in the face of change."

"Wow. It sounds like you think a lot of me," she teased to hide how his words warmed her soul.

"Aivier! Aivier!" The boys spotted him and came running. A foot away the two of them launched their little bodies in the air, hurtling themselves at Xavier. He caught the sturdy pair easily, tucking the pair under his arms and tickling mercilessly while the boys shrieked with laughter.

After a minute, he set them on their feet with a last tickle of their little bellies. Devin looked at Marcus and the two made another leap at Xavier. The game was repeated again, only this time they bulleted into her. Unprepared, she fell back under their weight, wincing as her hair fanned around her in the grass. That was going to be fun to comb out later.

Xavier loomed above her, ready to scoop the boys away,

but she shook her head, thrilling to the screams of laughter and joy until her mouth felt tired from smiling so big for so long. Then she wrapped the boys close and whispered, "Let's get Xavier."

Their eyes got big and they rolled to their feet. With evil smiles on their faces, they tiptoed toward where Xavier sat with a content look on his face, momentarily distracted by the phone in his hand. It made for the perfect ambush. Sensing something at the last moment, he looked up in time to brace himself for the twin attack. What he wasn't prepared for was for her to follow with a hard shove to his shoulders, and they all went tumbling to the ground.

The boys were instantly everywhere, digging in with their little fingers.

"I am not ticklish." The words rumbled in Xavier's chest under her ear. "But as I remember, you are."

In a heartbeat, the target changed from being Xavier to being her. Fingers, big and little, dug into her ribs, making her giggle. For a moment the sight of Xavier looming over her with a look of satisfaction shot her back to her bedroom in San Francisco when it was just the two of them snug in her bed, making love.

And when his eyes flashed with heat, the sense of longing the memory brought reached clear to her toes. She ruthlessly pushed it aside.

Instead she focused on the toddlers. She fought but the three of them were too much for her, tormenting her until tears rolled down her cheeks and she cried out for mercy.

"Stop! Stop!" she gasped.

Xavier relented, rolling to his feet and plucking the boys off her with a fist in the back of their shirts.

While Amanda lay recovering, the boys' nanny approached. She and Xavier exchanged words and he nodded. "It's time for them to go inside," he told Amanda. He kissed each boy on the cheek and then lowered them for her to give each boy a hug and a kiss.

The nanny took the boys in hand and led them inside. After watching to see the trio made it safely indoors, Xavier turned to offer her a hand.

Sad the happy interlude was over, she accepted and the hard yank he gave pulled her full into his arms.

She gasped and looked up ready to—

"We have an audience," he whispered, angling her slightly so she saw Carlo and Elayna walking together through the courtyard.

"I still say neither of them likes me," she muttered, feeling the dagger of their glares in her back.

"You exaggerate. Neither has reason to dislike you."

"Elayna does."

"She knows that it is over between us."

"Huh. Knowing and accepting are two different things. And Carlo always looks at me with suspicion in his eyes."

"That is Carlo. He senses there is something more to your visit and is frustrated that he is not in the know. Ignore him," he advised, his breath a caress across her cheek. "He cannot hurt you."

"It's not just me," she protested. "I don't want to cause trouble between my father and his people."

"Do not concern yourself. Your father knows how to deal with his people."

Carefully putting her back to the narrowed eyes of her nemeses, she pulled free of his unnerving embrace.

"I should get ready for the ball."

"Of course." He bowed his head in acknowledgement and bent to retrieve his jacket. "I will walk you inside."

She wanted to protest, but welcomed the distraction. With him at her side she was too bothered to wonder at her reaction to his impromptu embrace. She'd been ready to do something, but was it to lash out or latch on?

Rattled by the enforced intimacy and her shifting emotions, half the time she didn't know if she wanted to hit the man or kiss him.

CHAPTER FIFTEEN

BERNADETTE SENT A young maid to help Amanda prepare for the ball. She knocked just after Amanda climbed into her filmy undergarments.

A bit disconcerted she tried to send the girl away, but Collette insisted the Princess would be most displeased if she failed to assist Amanda in looking her best for the ball.

She held up a makeup case and a curling iron. "I do very nice things for the hair."

Hair was the magic word. Amanda opened the door wide and let the girl in. She'd been wondering what to do with her unruly mass of hair.

First Collette helped her into her dress and then Amanda sat and let the girl do her very nice things. She asked Amanda a few questions about her tastes, nodding at the honest answers then went to work.

"Oh my." Surveying her reflection in the mirror, Amanda caught her breath at the stunning picture she made. Strapless, the fitted bodice of the dress consisted of ruched panels with one panel at the breast and one over the hip, encrusted with silver beading. The back laced up like a corset and the skirt fell from the hips to the floor in a glimmering sweep of liquid silver. A short train gave the skirt a satisfying swish.

The makeup was subtle except for the mysterious shadowing Collette had given her eyes. And her hair Amanda sighed.

She'd swept the mass up into a sophisticated French twist, but of course there was too much hair, so from the top of the twist on down, the rest cascaded down her back in flowing curls. Tonight she truly felt like a princess.

"Collette, you have magic fingers. Thank you."

"It is easy when I have such beautiful hair and skin to work with. You are truly lovely." Collette finished packing up her tools and gave her a smile. "If you please, the Princess asked me to show you to the Blue Room when you were ready."

"Of course." Amanda checked her clutch and then followed the maid from the room.

"Enjoy the ball," the girl said a few minutes later after showing Amanda to a parlor beautifully appointed in shades of blue.

Not wanting to wrinkle her dress, she walked over to admire a painting of blue water lilies only to realize it was a genuine Monet. She blinked, experiencing an Alice-down-the-rabbit-hole moment. But then this whole week ranked as an out of reality experience.

She lifted her chin and drew her shoulders back, standing straight and tall. She'd handled it.

"Amanda."

Swinging around with a soft swish of her skirt, she found her father had joined her in the room. He wore a dark suit with a military cut and gold braiding over the shoulders, and his royal crest on the arm, looking every bit the prince he was.

"Papa," she greeted him with a kiss on the cheek. "How handsome you are."

"My dear, you take my breath away." He wrapped his arms around her, pulling her to him for a hug. She sank into the embrace, feeling both safe and cherished. This she realized was what she'd missed her whole life, a simple moment of closeness, a silent exchange of affection.

"I am so happy you came—" he pressed a kiss to her temple "—that we have had this time together."

"Me too." She stepped back, putting a finger to the corners of her eyes to catch the tears threatening to fall, before they could ruin her makeup. "I was just thinking how unreal much of this week has been. But the welcome you have all given me has been very real, very warm. Thank you."

"No thanks are necessary. You are family." He walked with her to a settee. "Amanda, I want you to know you are welcome to stay here. I will speak with my advisors this week and plan an announcement that you are my daughter."

"Oh. Really?" Flustered, she prattled with no thought behind her words. She took a breath and looked into his eyes. "I hadn't considered that option."

"I hope you will." He set a black velvet case on the table, to hold her hands. "I wish to acknowledge you as my daughter. You will never be in line to rule, but you will be an honored citizen."

"I don't know what to say." Except *Thank you God,* she'd never be in line to rule. She thought of her grandmother's ultimatum versus the warm welcome, the sense of family she'd found here. If she returned to the States, she may mend her relationship with her grandparents, but if she stayed, it was probably finished.

And then there was Michelle and Elle. Leaving them behind was unthinkable.

"Is it Xavier? He told me of your time together."

"He did?" Her eyes went big as her heart sank. She couldn't believe Xavier betrayed her again.

"No." He lifted the chin she'd lowered, forcing her to meet his gaze. "You must not blame him. I saw the way you clung to him and guessed there was more to it. He very reluctantly confirmed my suspicions. He held his silence much longer than I, his Ruler and your father, cared for."

"I'm not sure you get to be both at the same time." Did she get to be mad at Xavier for answering a direct question from his Prince? She didn't think so. She wouldn't lie to the President of the United States.

"But I am both."

"Not when it comes to my love life. Promise me there will be no politics, no persuasion, no undue pressure, no hint of a preference from you to Xavier regarding anything to do with me."

Clearly he did not care to have his hands tied. "I just want you to be happy."

"I know and I appreciate it, but my relationship with Xavier is over," she assured him, ignoring the mortifying heat in her cheeks in the hopes it would soon recede. "He ended it."

"And if he hadn't?"

Good question. She eyed him through her lashes. "He says we could never be together."

"Because he is a guard and you are—"

"Your daughter, yes. Is that true?"

For the first time since she met him, he didn't seem to have an answer. "I—I do not know. There is no precedent."

He stood and paced in front of the fireplace. She held her breath unsure why she let him struggle with the question when it didn't change anything. She'd given up on any future for her and Xavier. Hadn't she?

"I think in the past it may have been a problem, but these are modern times. Whether you agree to stay or only come for occasional visits you will be an honored citizen, and I would be most pleased if you found one of my people to make a life with."

"Oh, Papa." Such acceptance humbled her. "Then you need to let us find our own way. I cannot be with a man if I don't know that he is with me of his own free choice because he loves me."

"Of course he cares for you. Who would not love you?"

"Papa," she chided him, both pleased and exasperated. "It is not as simple between a man and a woman as between a father and daughter. But even in this short time I have also come to love you."

"Ah." He inclined his head to her. "A proud man does not always find it easy to express emotion. But you are smart as well as beautiful and you read me well. Yes, you have burrowed your way into my heart. I will be quite distressed if we were to become separated again."

"Me too," she said softly. "Papa, how did your relationship with my mother end? Did she just leave at the end of the summer?" He'd told her much of her mother, but not this.

"There are times when you look so much like her it takes me back twenty-five years. Those were not my best years. I was arrogant and felt entitled. And I was hurting, as it seemed certain I would lose my grandmother." He led her back to the sofa, urged her to sit.

"Haley made all that go away. When her time to leave Pasadonia came, I asked her to stay and she did, allowing her friends to travel on to Italy without her. I believe she wrote letters to her parents and had her friends mail them for her. She never liked to talk about them much."

"But she returned with her friends to the United States."

"*Oui.* Again I asked her to stay, but I could not give her assurances of a future together. I was not ready to settle down. I could not think of such with my grandmother's illness."

"You never tried to find her?"

"I had no reason to. Life moved on. If I had known of you, I would have stopped at nothing to find you."

"I know." She believed him. Believed also that her mother had lacked the courage to reach for forbidden love so far from everything she knew.

If given the chance, would she have the guts to do what her mother hadn't?

"Enough of this seriousness." He walked to the table and picked up the black case. "I came to give you this." Lifting the top, he revealed a glittering diamond necklace. A web of descending scallops ending in a teardrop diamond as big as her thumbnail.

"It was Vivienne's. It seems appropriate you should have it."

"Oh, no." A hand to her throat, Amanda stepped away. "I couldn't possibly."

"I want you to wear it." He lifted the jewels from the case.

"Bernadette," she said helplessly.

"She agrees these will look beautiful on you."

"Someone may recognize them," she argued, even as she stopped her retreat.

"Doubtful. The only portrait of her wearing the jewels has been on tour for nearly six months."

"That's right." She remembered the piece now. "This necklace was on the tour. I saw it in San Francisco."

"I had it flown back just for tonight."

"Goodness, I guess I can't let that extravagance go to waste."

"Excellent." He had her turn and fastened the clasp. Then he walked her to a gold-framed mirror. "Absolutely stunning. No doubt about it. You will be the belle of the ball."

Amanda slowly made her way to the ball. Her father had given her much to think about. Not least of which was clearing the way for her and Xavier to be together. Would he be pleased by the news or find another excuse for them to break up?

And how did she feel? Did she want another chance with Xavier?

The sharp spike of lust and longing she'd experienced in

the courtyard earlier surely indicated yes. The simple truth was she loved him.

And she missed him.

All week he'd been close by, either keeping an eye on her and the kids, or her and the Princess, or escorting her to some event or another. Those were especially trying times, when he actually touched her. How bittersweet to have him hold her hand or drape an arm around her shoulders when she knew it was just for show.

She wanted to go back in time to when they were a couple and pretend the breakup never happened. But she hadn't played make-believe since the year Grandmother refused to let her go back to Princess Camp.

So the question remained, did she love him enough to put the past behind them and move forward together? Assuming he even wanted her.

Who was she kidding? She knew he wanted her. The flash of heat in his eyes today, the way his hands lingered on her longer then circumstances warranted, and his overstimulated protective instincts made it clear. He couldn't hide his feelings any better than he could lie to his Prince. Honor and honesty were built into his DNA.

Being so hurt she'd lost sight of that for a while. Not anymore. She had a future to plan and where he fit into it played a big part in the decisions she had to make.

Reaching the top of the staircase leading to the foyer of the ballroom, Xavier suddenly came into view. He waited to the right of the entrance, out of the flow of traffic.

Her breath caught in her chest. He looked magnificent in his dress uniform of black trousers and white jacket, with braiding and medals draped and pinned on him to show his rank and mettle. He stood as tall and proud as any Prince Charming she had ever read about.

But this princess had found her prince in her father and now she just wanted an ordinary man, to live an ordinary life.

No, she corrected as she walked toward her future, an extraordinary man to live an extraordinary life.

His eyes gleamed his approval when she reached him. He bent over her hand, kissing the backs of her fingers.

"Never have I seen anything more beautiful than you in this dress. You are a moonbeam sent down from heaven."

Pleased, she beamed up at him and ran a proprietary hand along his lapel. "I feel beautiful tonight. You look gorgeous yourself. I'm going to have to find a stick so I can fight the girls away."

"I have eyes for no one but you." He tucked her arm into the crook of his elbow and led her inside. "You must save every dance for me."

Hearing their names announced together gave her a thrill and set the tone of the evening. After proceeding through the receiving line where she exchanged warm glances with her father and Bernadette and wary gazes with Carlo, Xavier led her through the glittering crowd to a cocktail table where his parents stood with drinks waiting.

There would be no sitting in the ballroom, but a few salons opened off the east wall and the terrace doors were open, inviting the guests to enjoy the evening air.

"My dear, you are simply enchanting." Yvette greeted her with a kiss on each cheek.

Philippe also claimed a kiss as Amanda admired Yvette, the woman's lush curves shown to advantage in a scooped neck midnight blue gown that belled gently from a dropped waist.

"This room is spectacular." Amanda turned in a complete circle to take in the huge room framed by elaborate molding in antique gold, while white marble columns marched in matched pairs down the length of the room, separated by side tables topped by white rose bouquets bigger than she was. Three crystal chandeliers glimmered overhead and a dropped balcony housed a full orchestra. A lovely stage for the festive attendees dressed in lavish gowns, slick tuxedos and sparkling jewels.

"I love these affairs," Yvette confessed. "It is the one night of the year I feel important."

"My dear." Philippe pulled her close and planted a kiss in the curls piled on top of her head. "You are important to me every day of the year."

"Mon amour." She gave him a loving glance and he took the opportunity to steal a kiss.

Amanda sighed. Such love after being together for more than thirty years. That's what she wanted.

"I know what Yvette means. Tonight has a special feel to it, a fairytale feel." She lifted her glass of champagne. "So I propose a toast, to happily ever after."

"Perfect." Yvette gave a delighted laugh. And Xavier and Philippe indulged her by clinking glasses.

Music swelled through the room and Jean Claude and Bernadette took to the floor to start the dancing. When other couples joined them, Xavier held his hand out to her and inclined his head in invitation.

Placing her hand in his, she followed him to the dance floor and flowed into his arms. Time flew after that as the music moved from one piece to the next and she danced with one charming partner after another—including her father for a few brief minutes, and for which she received a fierce glare of disapproval from Carlo.

Xavier seemed content to watch her, taking to the floor only a few times. Once with his mother and a couple of times with women who were obviously friends of his mother's. When Elayna asked him, he politely declined.

Seeing the exchange, Amanda smiled brightly at her current partner, and pleading the need for some air, excused herself. Once free of him, she threaded her way back to Xavier, who immediately opened his arms and moved them into a slow waltz.

Yes. She sighed and relaxed against him, letting him lead them through the crush. For a few minutes she just enjoyed the moment. The lilting music, the ambiance, the solid feel of his arms around her.

Had there ever been a more perfect moment?

Except it wasn't perfect was it, if he was only here out of a sense of duty?

Enough already. She was tired of wondering, tired of almost being with him. She needed to know how he really felt, and not just what was expected of him.

Lifting her head, she met his intense gaze and hope swelled within her. Surely that much heat must have some feeling behind it.

"Who would you be with tonight, if you weren't required to put on this act with me?"

His dark brows lowered into a frown. "I am not now, nor have I ever put on an act when I was with you. And I would not wish to be here with anyone but you."

"Truly?"

"Truly."

"Who did you come with last year?"

"I came alone last year." He gave a half smile. "I was a great hit with my mother's friends."

"It's very sweet of you to dance with them. I'm sure it's the highlight of their night."

"Hmm." He swung her around, tightening his arm around her waist and pulling her tighter to him. "Does this interest in my past activities mean you've forgiven me?"

She tilted her head to gaze up at him. "Why do you want

my forgiveness when you've chosen not to fight for any future together?"

"I have been rethinking my decision. Having you so close this week but not being able to really talk to you, share your laughter, has shredded my heart every minute of every day."

The rawness of his voice ripped right through any lingering doubts. She threaded her fingers in the crisp softness of his hair and pulled his head down to hers. With a hoarse groan he closed the distance between them, claiming her mouth as if starved for the taste of her.

And she savored his ardor because it had been forever since she felt the press of his lips, the sweep of his tongue, since she drank in the very essence of him. But after a moment she pulled back. It wasn't going to be that easy.

"So I should forgive you? But you were just doing your job, fulfilling your duty to your Prince and your country?"

"Yes. But I was clumsy about it and my actions hurt you. For this I am sorry."

"Because I was too much temptation for you?"

He lifted a dark eyebrow and his gaze roved over her cleavage, her bare shoulders, her hair, before he looked her square in the eyes. She expected a playful lob, but he gave her total capitulation.

"Yes," he confessed. "You stole my ability to think clearly."

Oh she liked that. This confrontation may not be as bad as she thought. Still, he deserved a little torture for the heartache she suffered while he was being stubborn.

"So you're saying it was my fault?"

"Yes."

She lifted both brows at him.

"I mean, no." He quickly backpedalled. "Of course not."

When she smiled brightly, he narrowed stern eyes at her. "You are playing with me."

She blinked innocent eyes. "Would I do that?"

"Yes. I do believe you have a bit of a vixen in you." He tightened his grip on her waist, hauling her closer and bowing his head to whisper in her ear, "I like it."

And she liked the way his breath tickled her skin. Angling her head up, she nipped at his jaw then kissed it better. He made a noise deep in his throat and then his mouth was on hers, claiming her as his in a kiss just short of savage.

With a hum of approval she surrendered to his unleashed passion, standing pliant in the wake of his ravishing demand. Giving so he didn't have to take, receiving such intense pleasure, she trembled with the need for more.

The press of his body against hers revealed his desire equaled hers. He finally lifted his head enough to drag his mouth to her ear. "Have mercy."

She gave him a closed-mouth smile, took his hand and headed for the door.

CHAPTER SIXTEEN

AMANDA STOOD WITH Xavier saying their goodbyes to Yvette and Philippe when suddenly trumpets blared and into the following silence two names were announced, Philippe and Xavier. She noticed the LeDuc family seemed surprised but happy.

With a squeeze of her hand, Xavier left her to join his father to walk to the front of the room where marble steps led to a raised section where her father and Bernadette sat in elaborate thrones. The night took on even more of a fairytale aspect as she followed an excited Yvette in the men's wake.

"What's going on?" she asked, once the two of them stood ringside at the bottom of the stairs where the men stood shoulder to shoulder. Xavier was by far the youngest of the group.

"The men are being knighted," Yvette whispered. "It is the highest honor a guard can achieve. He must be proficient with three weapons, have acquired ten citations, and have the recommendation of three superior officers. Many years we have no candidates. I have never known of a father and son being knighted in the same ceremony." Tears spilled from her brown eyes. "I am so proud."

A gentleman with a chest full of medals and a sleeve full of stripes stepped forward and recited the list of Philippe's and Xavier's accomplishments, which took some time but

was thankfully done in English as the many visiting dignitaries made it the most common language.

Finally her father rose and came forward. A page followed
with a large sword balanced on a velvet pillow. Once Jean
Claude reached center stage Philippe and Xavier climbed the
stairs and knelt in front of him.

Pride swelled in Amanda. Xavier had worked so hard for
this. For a few moments she'd feared her father might have
interfered by preempting Xavier into the honor because of
her. Xavier would hate that, as would she. But as his qualifi-
cations were announced there was no doubt he'd earned this
prestigious acknowledgement all on his own.

And with that realization came another. She had to let her
anger go. How could she blame him for acting like a soldier
when that was exactly what he was? He may have harbored
secret hopes for another occupation at one time, but that only
inspired him to dig deeper, try harder, push himself more.

She got it now. The fact he allowed the man inside to rear
his head at all was a huge compliment. That's what his mother
had been trying to tell her.

No wonder he found it hard to communicate his feelings
to her. He had no experience dealing with them. The one relationship that even came close was due to a family connection from his youth.

Well, he was just going to have to suck it up, because she
needed to hear how he felt. From him.

With great ceremony her father tapped Xavier on the right
shoulder and spoke of his great skill with weapons, then he
tapped the left shoulder and commended him on his strong
heart and loyalty, last he tapped him on the head and reminded Xavier of his eternal duty to crown and country. The
same was repeated with Philippe, and then Jean Claude bid
them to rise as Sir Xavier and Sir Philippe, Royal Knights
of Pasadonia.

Amanda clapped so hard her hands stung, and once the music started again, making it obvious the ceremony was over, she rushed forward to claim her man.

When he saw her, he moved to meet her halfway, pulling her into his arms and stepping into the dance in one smooth move.

"Congratulations." She threw her arms around his neck. "Sir Xavier."

"I don't forgive you." Lying sated in Xavier's arms, Amanda felt his body go completely still.

She'd never answered his question and now she rolled over to prop herself on his chest and look down into his amber eyes. "Because there is nothing to forgive. I finally got it tonight, Sir Xavier. Being a guard isn't something you do, it's who you are. You couldn't have acted any differently than you did."

"I have thought about what you said on the plane, and though I have never considered another direction in my life, it is possible an interest in engineering caused me to over-compensate in my dedication to duty. It was never a problem until you." He relaxed back against the mattress and lifted a hand to gently brush her hair away from her face. "I should have handled it better."

"I'm glad you didn't, because that might mean we wouldn't have had the time together that we did. And I wouldn't give up those memories for anything."

He crunched up to give her a kiss. "Me, neither. I promise to always be honest with you. By your definition."

She smiled at that. "I love you."

Again he froze, his chest not even lifting with air. A hundred years passed. And then his fingers tunneled through her hair and he pulled her over him to plunder her mouth with exquisite tenderness. And as her heart still raced and her chest heaved for breath, she heard the mumbled words, "I love you."

Smiling, she slid into sleep. He loved her. The rest they could figure out tomorrow.

Xavier was gone when Amanda woke in the morning, but he'd left a note on his pillow inviting her to lunch with him and his family.

A glance at the clock showed the time was later than she thought. If she wanted to play with the twins before meeting Xavier, she'd have to rush.

Carlo had left a voice message for her to come see him before doing anything. She shook her head. Not without Xavier, so that would have to wait.

She dressed in cream linen pants and a silk sweater and hurried out to the courtyard. She waved to the nanny who gave her an odd look. She wondered about that but the twins spotted her. The boys were thrilled to see her and clamored all over her. And she learned the lesson of wearing light clothes around little boys.

Deciding the clothes were replaceable but her brothers' kisses weren't, she finished playing and gave them hugs before returning to her room to change.

As she was running late, she texted Xavier she'd meet him in the front drive to the palace, which was a closer walk from her rooms than to the garage.

In the front foyer she hitched her purse over her shoulder and waved at the guards standing sentinel.

"Miss." One of the guards moved to intercept her. "There is a lot of press out front. You may want to use another exit."

"Oh, I'm sure it'll be fine." She gave him a self-deprecating smile. "I'm nobody."

He did not return her smile but simply stated, "I will step out with you."

"That's not necessary. I'm just meeting Commandant LeDuc in the curve."

"I will escort you."

"Thank you." Giving in to his determination, she gracefully allowed him to walk her outside.

They were about ten feet from the door when the cry went out.

"Amanda Carn! It's her." A crowd of bodies rushed her.

"Amanda, what is your purpose for being in Pasadonia?"

"Mademoiselle!"

"Amanda!"

"How do you know the Prince?"

"Vous êtes la maitresse du Prince?"

Bombarded with questions in a variety of languages, only half of which she understood, she froze. Had someone just asked if she was Jean Claude's mistress? This was horrible.

The guard immediately put himself between her and the pack. Over his shoulder he instructed her to head back to the door.

She tried, shuffling sideways, but the pack surged closer and she shrank back. Her stomach burned with dread. Fear weighted her down.

This was bad.

"Over here, Amanda!"

"Mademoiselle Carn, what is your relationship with the Prince?"

This was worse, far worse, than tripping around campus worried about staining her grandparents' reputations. Yes, her grandparents' careers were important and could have suffered from any inappropriate actions on her part, but a campus was small potatoes next to a country and a professor's reputation just didn't weigh in at the international level. She could do real damage to her father's credibility.

Just the thought made the blood run cold in her veins.

And it didn't end there. Xavier and his family would suffer from their association with her. This was a nightmare.

"Amanda."

"Mademoiselle."

"Amanda."

Amanda made no effort to respond. Overwhelmed by the unexpectedness of the attack, her mind just kept looping why? Another guard arrived and helped to hold back the horde, but she was so distraught and disoriented she stood frozen in place.

"Amanda, are you the Prince's daughter?"

"Ms. Carn! This way. Is the Prince your papa?"

She flinched at the questions. How had they found out? She must have made a mistake. The guards urged her to move, but her mind raced. What had she done? Where? When?

And then Xavier was there, wrapping a hard arm around her waist, lifting her against his chest, and hustling her inside. Even as she buried her face against him, more guards arrived, moving outside to remove the press, still calling questions through the door.

"Are you okay? You are shaking."

"They know," she said into his chest. She'd never been so happy for his strength than in that moment. "How can they know? I must have done something wrong."

"Shh." He soothed a hand over her hair. "You did nothing wrong."

"Mademoiselle Carn." Carlo's voice boomed through the foyer. "You will come with me."

She cringed, and Xavier's arms tightened around her. He put himself between her and the Social Secretary. She loved him so much she realized she needed to pull it together for him. And for her father. The news was out. It was time to deal with it.

Pulling free of Xavier's comforting embrace, she lifted her chin and faced Carlo.

"Let's go."

Amanda's distress ate at Xavier from his stance in the corner. He felt helpless as Carlo ranted about a picture of Amanda and Jean Claude dancing at the ball, appearing on an internet blog with a post from an anonymous source asking who the upstart American was and what was her relationship to the Prince of Pasadonia? Surely for anyone to get that close to the Prince she had to be his mistress or a long lost daughter.

He went on to state the whole incident with the press could have been avoided if she had come to see him as he requested.

"I'm sorry," she apologized for the third time. "But if you had given me some indication of what you needed to see me about, I could have made an informed decision."

"There should be no decision. I am the Social Secretary. I do not make frivolous summons."

Her chin tipped up. "And I'm an American citizen not subject to summons."

Good for her. Xavier welcomed the anger in her eyes. She'd deal better with a little fire in her blood. He felt comfortable enough to text the security office and request they trace the anonymous poster.

Carlo seemed more interested in crucifying Amanda than in finding who instigated the problem. Elayna, who stood quietly to the left of Carlo's desk, had contributed nothing so far. Her avid expression reflected no compassion for Amanda.

"You are a guest in our country." Carlo raked Xavier with a disapproving glance. "You have overstepped yourself on more than one occasion. Now you have created a scandal that has embarrassed the Prince. Your actions are unacceptable."

Xavier stepped forward. "Your tone is unacceptable."

"Keep out of this, LeDuc, or I will have you removed from

this office. You should be more concerned with how this affects the Prince than this woman."

"The Prince should be here." Xavier pulled his phone out again and pushed a button.

"The Prince has been apprised of the situation," Carlo said quickly. "I am handling this."

"Jean Claude," Xavier said into the phone. "You are needed in Carlo's office. It's about Amanda." He flipped the phone closed. "He will be here in a few minutes."

"That was unnecessary." Carlo was livid. "The remedy to this is simple. Once Miss Carn is gone, the scandal will leave with her."

"That is not an acceptable resolution," Xavier stated.

"He's right, Xavier," Amanda spoke up. "If my presence is causing trouble for Jean Claude, I need to leave."

"We will let Jean Claude decide what should be done."

"Damn you, LeDuc. I could have handled this."

"By banishing her?" Xavier mocked him. "You should be thanking me. I just saved you from yourself. Have you made any effort to find who posted to the blog?" he demanded. "It had to be someone at the ball. You should be focusing your ire in that direction, not on Amanda."

The door swung open and Jean Claude marched inside, followed by Bernadette.

"Carlo," Jean Claude addressed his Social Secretary. "What is going on here?"

Carlo explained the situation, making it clear his earlier claim of doing so had been false.

"My dear, are you okay?" Jean Claude's first concern was for his daughter.

"Yes," Amanda assured him. "I'm sorry."

"You have nothing to apologize for." Bernadette came forward to take her hand. "I know how traumatic it is to be besieged by the press."

Jean Claude moved the second visitor chair over so Bernadette could sit next to Amanda.

"What have you found out about the blog poster?" Jean Claude followed the same thought process as Xavier. "I will not tolerate a guest of mine insulting me in this manner. It should be a simple matter for Security to trace."

"Of course, Your Highness." Carlo cleared his throat. "I will follow up immediately. I felt it best to deal with Miss Carn first. The allegations of the press are ridiculous but the attention you have given her has obviously been misconstrued. It is best if she cuts her visit short."

"That is not your call."

"Jean Claude." Bernadette's tone urged the Prince to calm himself. "I believe it is time to announce who Amanda is. It is the only thing that will hush the speculations."

"You are right, as usual." Jean Claude claimed his wife's hand and kissed her knuckles. He flicked his gaze to Carlo. "Put together a press conference for this afternoon."

"I do not understand," the Social Secretary protested. "What will you be announcing?"

"Amanda is my daughter."

"Your daughter!" Carlo's voice held the shrillness of a damp cat. "Why was I not told of this? I am the Social Secretary. I could have managed this with some dignity."

"Nobody knew of this. I wanted some time to get to know Amanda before it was made public." Jean Claude went on to explain the situation. "However, it is time to advise the whole council. Please arrange an emergency meeting. I want a plan in place before the press conference at three."

"What of LeDuc's involvement?" Carlo made notes on an open pad on his desk. "I assume the relationship was a cover for her presence here."

Amanda made a distressed noise in the back of her throat.

"The relationship is real," Xavier stated with authority. He caught the Prince's gaze and decided to make his position totally clear. "Your Highness, I would like to speak to you later about marrying your daughter."

Jean Claude gave a nod of approval.

Carlo had a fit. "Marriage! You need to slow down. There are precedents and politics to consider."

"Stop! Just stop." Amanda sprang from her seat. "You don't have to worry. There's not going to be any marriage." Xavier's gut clenched at the anguished gaze she shot him before including Jean Claude in her focus.

She waved toward Carlo. "He's right, and this is exactly what the country's reaction is going to be. The press had the same response. I'm an interloper, trying to force my way in where I'm not wanted. I don't want to cause anyone any more embarrassment. Or hurt anyone by being associated with me. It's best if I leave."

"No." Jean Claude moved to her side and pulled her into a warm hug. "I always intended to tell the people. It is unfortunate you had to suffer this unpleasantness before I could claim you."

"No, Papa." Amanda pushed away. "Carlo is right. I've just caused trouble. I will always treasure our time together, but it's time for me to go."

And she rushed from the room.

Xavier immediately made to follow her and found himself shoulder to shoulder with Jean Claude. The older man met his gaze and inclined his head, indicating Xavier should go after Amanda. "Convince her to stay."

Amanda raced through the halls of the palace, seeking the sanctuary of her rooms. She probably provided quite the picture for the security cameras, bumbling along, tears staining her cheeks. But the need for discretion was gone. Their secret was out, an ugly blotch on the Prince's reputation.

This whole mess was her fault. She had to make it right, and the best way to do that was to remove herself so the scandal could just fade away. She refused to cause the people she loved and cared about any more damage or embarrassment.

And she really had come to love her family here; she honestly felt like a member of a real, caring family. But she'd been a fool to think it could last.

In her suite, she pulled out her cell to call Michelle or Elle, but the time caught her eye and she realized it was the middle of the night back home. She flipped the phone closed, grabbed the box of tissues, and stepped out onto the balcony overlooking the courtyard.

She had to make travel arrangements, but she needed a few minutes first or she'd be a sobbing mess trying to talk to the airlines.

In spite of being at odds with Xavier, this last week included some of the happiest days of her life. And just when they finally found their way back together, this happened.

Obviously they weren't meant to be.

Strong arms wrapped around her and pulled her back against a hard chest. Instant recognition had her hugging his arms to her. She dug her nails into the fabric of his jacket, both comforted and upset by his appearance.

"You aren't going to change my mind. I've caused enough damage here."

"Sweetheart, you are in shock from a traumatic event. There is no need for me to change your mind. Once you have had time to calm down and put the incident into perspective, you will see for yourself that you have done nothing wrong. There is no need for you to go anywhere."

"But—"

"No buts. Just let me hold you for a few minutes. Do not think, just breathe with me."

Because it was easier to give in than to fight, she relaxed

against him, breathed as he breathed. And slowly felt the tension fade away.

Xavier's phone buzzed. He moved one arm to answer, listened for a few minutes, grunting once as his body went taut. "I will tell her. I am working on it. Of course." He disconnected, returned the phone to his pocket, and his arm around her.

"My father?"

"Yes. He wanted to know if I had convinced you to stay and whether I still wanted to speak with him this afternoon."

"And what are you to tell me?" She couldn't deal with the other yet.

"Elayna was the anonymous blogger. She confessed after I left the room. She was jealous of you and thought if she caused you trouble, you would leave. She had no idea you were actually the Prince's daughter."

"I told you she didn't like me."

"It appears you were right. I am sorry. I should have noticed her antipathy sooner. I let old ties blind me."

"Stop." She moved to face him, ran a finger down his chiseled jaw. "You are not responsible for her bad behavior. So just cool your guilt engines."

"You do not blame me for her leaking you to the world?"

Leaking? She bit back a grin. She really shouldn't laugh in the face of his sincere concern. His English was so good, these odd moments could lead to totally inappropriate reactions.

"How could you suspect her of such a thing? I don't like the woman, and I would never have thought her capable of betraying the Prince."

"She did not think of it as such. The Prince is often the target of gossip. She figured this would be no different but that you would suffer the inconvenience of the press pestering you for the remainder of your stay."

"That's messed up."

"Yes, she messed up. None of this is your fault. I want you to stay."

"But—"

He pressed a finger to her lips. "No buts. If you do not find blame for me, you cannot blame yourself for Elayna's actions, either."

"Maybe not." She'd cooled off enough to see the sense of that. "But my part in this is more complex than yours. Jean Claude is talking to his advisors. He's planning to make an announcement to the people. Everything is going to change, and I don't know that I'm ready."

"I am here to help you. There is nothing we cannot handle together."

She tried a smile. "That sounds pretty good." But if she stayed, if she became known as the Prince's daughter, incidents with the press would become a part of her life.

And that frightened her. Forever more her actions would reflect on her father. On Xavier.

She'd just gained her freedom at home. If she stayed, she'd be giving it up for good. Their lives would always be under the scrutiny of the paparazzi.

"The press scared you," he guessed.

She nodded, ducking her head.

But he wouldn't let her hide; a finger under her chin lifted her gaze to his. And there was so much love for her shining there, her breath caught in her chest.

A good thing, because he lowered his head and kissed her, claiming her mouth with tenderness and care. He made her feel cherished, loved.

"I will not lie. The press can be tough, but you can learn to handle them so they become less scary." He pressed his forehead to hers. "What you cannot do is give them power over you. I know how much you missed in life growing up in the shadow of your grandparents, of your mother."

Something loosened in her heart at his words. It showed how well he got her.

"You have found a family here that loves you. I love you." Oh God, she needed to hear that. "Are you going to let a little scare chase you away?"

Was she?

She'd longed for a family for so long, had wondered who her father was and she'd found both here in Pasadonia. Was she going to run because loving them was going to require that she step outside her ivory tower?

He swept her up, holding her against his chest so they were lip to lip, eye to eye. She felt like she was floating as she looked into his eyes.

"So you will stay? Marry me. Have my children."

Overcome with love, with happiness for all she'd gained by taking a chance on this man, she couldn't speak for a moment. Her throat closed with the force of her emotions.

Undeterred, he looked her straight in the eyes. "Amanda, the only question there was if we stay or return to America. I will have you for my wife. You will be the mother of my children. It's just a matter of where we live."

Okay she knew she should be upset by his arrogance, but truthfully it was so hot to be wanted that strongly.

"You would leave Pasadonia for me?"

"Of course. I love you."

"But your family is here. Your career. You can't just quit the militia."

"Amanda, you are my future, wherever you are is where I will be. And whether you are here or in America, the Prince will want you protected. I will have no problem working out my current commission."

How simple he made it sound.

"If you are worried about missing Michelle and Elle, let me remind you your father has his own jet."

He knew her so well. And she knew him as well. His willingness to leave Pasadonia told her how much he truly loved her. She could never let him make that big a sacrifice.

"Do not make me bring in the big guns," he whispered in her ear. "I can have the twins here in a matter of minutes."

She laughed and looped her arms around his neck. "You play dirty." She sighed and let the last of her worries drain away. Smiling against his mouth, she said, "You win. I'll marry you."

And then she rocked back on her heels and made her demands. "I want my wedding in the palace with both Michelle and Elle there. I deserve some reward for putting up with the press."

"I can make that happen." He didn't even hesitate. "I know this guy…"

"My hero." She pulled his head down and kissed him.

EPILOGUE

One year later

AMANDA STOOD IN the vestibule of the palace chapel watching as Xavier's sister started down the aisle. Lovely in a strapless aqua mermaid dress, she led the procession, with Elle following in a matching yellow dress, and then Michelle in pink. The colors of their princess dresses from years ago at Princess Camp.

Fanciful, yes. But Amanda thought it appropriate considering it turned out she really was a princess. Okay, not technically. But close enough.

Her friends looked beautiful, especially Michelle, who was radiant in her fourth month of pregnancy. And Elle still had the sparkle of a newlywed. The three of them had worked out a round robin so each of them was the maid or matron of honor for one of the others.

Between the internet and Papa's jet, she barely missed them at all.

Of course she had so much family now with Papa, Bernadette and the twins, but more so she had Xavier's family. His mother and sister immediately swept her into the fold, and it had been great fun learning all Xavier's secrets.

She'd been worried how the public would react to her existence, but the whole country had welcomed her. The Prince's relationship with her mother was seen as a tragic love story while his reconciliation with Amanda was looked on as a happy circumstance of the romantic tale.

Her engagement to Xavier, a decorated officer of the Royal Republican Guard, played like a fairy tale in the press.

She could live with that.

She couldn't wait to live with him. Being such a public figure this last year, she'd insisted on keeping separate living arrangements. Which didn't mean they hadn't found time to be together. He often discreetly made his way to her rooms. Still she longed to move into the house they'd chosen together and start her life with him.

"Are you ready?" Papa laid his hand over hers on his sleeve.

"Yes." She glanced at him so handsome and proud.

"Nervous?" He smiled at her.

"Not in the least. Thank you for the beautiful wedding. It's beyond what I ever dreamed of."

"You are beyond anything I ever dreamed of. I'm so glad I found you." He tipped her face up to kiss her cheek. "And now I have to give you away."

"He'll take good care of me. And I'm not going far."

"He'd better." A glint entered his eyes. "I'll be watching him."

"Papa."

His brows lowered. "I know. No interference. You make it hard on a Prince."

"Then just be my papa."

He pursed his lips and looked ahead. "This is no easier."

She laughed. "Then just love me."

He brightened. "This I can do."

She squeezed his arm and together they started down the aisle. Music swelled and the attendees all stood in honor of the bride. The chapel had been dressed in white and gold with lots of greenery and fresh roses and hundreds of candles lit on crystal pedestals making the room twinkle like a fairy bower.

Near the front she spied her grandparents. Grandfather, it turned out, overrode Grandmother's ultimatum and made it clear he intended to remain a part of Amanda's life. He'd urged her to call whenever she was on the West Coast so he could arrange to see her. Grandmother had come around when the wedding invitation arrived, offering a stay in the palace.

In a world turned upside down, Amanda found it reassuring that some things never changed.

And then there Xavier was, standing at the front of the church, magnificent in his dress uniform complete with sword. Thrilled at the sight of him, she smiled. How she loved him.

Every minute of every day was better because he was a part of her life.

His intense gaze met hers as if her veil were mere mist. He didn't smile, didn't flinch. His gaze was steady and sure and a little impatient. She read him loud and clear. He wanted her, wanted this over so she would be his forever.

She couldn't agree more.

She spoke the truth when she told Papa Xavier would take good care of her. He already did. He treated her with the respect of a partner. Lavished her with the passion of a lover. And loved her as a man cherished his woman.

Her father gave her hand to Xavier and without hesitation she curled her fingers around his. The priest took them through the ceremony and she recited her vows to Xavier, but spoke loud enough for all to hear of her love and devotion to this exceptional man. He said his vows as if speaking just to her, uncaring who else heard his pledge.

"I now pronounce you man and wife. You may kiss the bride."

Xavier immediately crowded close, lifting her veil. And

now the smile came as he lowered his head. "I love you, Mrs. LeDuc."

And he claimed her with a searing kiss.

* * * * *

Mills & Boon® Hardback
June 2013

ROMANCE

The Sheikh's Prize — Lynne Graham
Forgiven but not Forgotten? — Abby Green
His Final Bargain — Melanie Milburne
A Throne for the Taking — Kate Walker
Diamond in the Desert — Susan Stephens
A Greek Escape — Elizabeth Power
Princess in the Iron Mask — Victoria Parker
An Invitation to Sin — Sarah Morgan
Too Close for Comfort — Heidi Rice
The Right Mr Wrong — Natalie Anderson
The Making of a Princess — Teresa Carpenter
Marriage for Her Baby — Raye Morgan
The Man Behind the Pinstripes — Melissa McClone
Falling for the Rebel Falcon — Lucy Gordon
Secrets & Saris — Shoma Narayanan
The First Crush Is the Deepest — Nina Harrington
One Night She Would Never Forget — Amy Andrews
When the Cameras Stop Rolling... — Connie Cox

MEDICAL

NYC Angels: Making the Surgeon Smile — Lynne Marshall
NYC Angels: An Explosive Reunion — Alison Roberts
The Secret in His Heart — Caroline Anderson
The ER's Newest Dad — Janice Lynn

Mills & Boon® Large Print
June 2013

ROMANCE

Sold to the Enemy	Sarah Morgan
Uncovering the Silveri Secret	Melanie Milburne
Bartering Her Innocence	Trish Morey
Dealing Her Final Card	Jennie Lucas
In the Heat of the Spotlight	Kate Hewitt
No More Sweet Surrender	Caitlin Crews
Pride After Her Fall	Lucy Ellis
Her Rocky Mountain Protector	Patricia Thayer
The Billionaire's Baby SOS	Susan Meier
Baby out of the Blue	Rebecca Winters
Ballroom to Bride and Groom	Kate Hardy

HISTORICAL

Never Trust a Rake	Annie Burrows
Dicing with the Dangerous Lord	Margaret McPhee
Haunted by the Earl's Touch	Ann Lethbridge
The Last de Burgh	Deborah Simmons
A Daring Liaison	Gail Ranstrom

MEDICAL

From Christmas to Eternity	Caroline Anderson
Her Little Spanish Secret	Laura Iding
Christmas with Dr Delicious	Sue MacKay
One Night That Changed Everything	Tina Beckett
Christmas Where She Belongs	Meredith Webber
His Bride in Paradise	Joanna Neil

0513 GEN STD LP

Mills & Boon® Hardback

July 2013

ROMANCE

His Most Exquisite Conquest	Emma Darcy
One Night Heir	Lucy Monroe
His Brand of Passion	Kate Hewitt
The Return of Her Past	Lindsay Armstrong
The Couple who Fooled the World	Maisey Yates
Proof of Their Sin	Dani Collins
In Petrakis's Power	Maggie Cox
A Shadow of Guilt	Abby Green
Once is Never Enough	Mira Lyn Kelly
The Unexpected Wedding Guest	Aimee Carson
A Cowboy To Come Home To	Donna Alward
How to Melt a Frozen Heart	Cara Colter
The Cattleman's Ready-Made Family	Michelle Douglas
Rancher to the Rescue	Jennifer Faye
What the Paparazzi Didn't See	Nicola Marsh
My Boyfriend and Other Enemies	Nikki Logan
The Gift of a Child	Sue MacKay
How to Resist a Heartbreaker	Louisa George

MEDICAL

Dr Dark and Far-Too Delicious	Carol Marinelli
Secrets of a Career Girl	Carol Marinelli
A Date with the Ice Princess	Kate Hardy
The Rebel Who Loved Her	Jennifer Taylor

0613 GEN STD HB

ROMANCE

Playing the Dutiful Wife	Carol Marinelli
The Fallen Greek Bride	Jane Porter
A Scandal, a Secret, a Baby	Sharon Kendrick
The Notorious Gabriel Diaz	Cathy Williams
A Reputation For Revenge	Jennie Lucas
Captive in the Spotlight	Annie West
Taming the Last Acosta	Susan Stephens
Guardian to the Heiress	Margaret Way
Little Cowgirl on His Doorstep	Donna Alward
Mission: Soldier to Daddy	Soraya Lane
Winning Back His Wife	Melissa McClone

HISTORICAL

The Accidental Prince	Michelle Willingham
The Rake to Ruin Her	Julia Justiss
The Outrageous Belle Marchmain	Lucy Ashford
Taken by the Border Rebel	Blythe Gifford
Unmasking Miss Lacey	Isabelle Goddard

MEDICAL

The Surgeon's Doorstep Baby	Marion Lennox
Dare She Dream of Forever?	Lucy Clark
Craving Her Soldier's Touch	Wendy S. Marcus
Secrets of a Shy Socialite	Wendy S. Marcus
Breaking the Playboy's Rules	Emily Forbes
Hot-Shot Doc Comes to Town	Susan Carlisle